With love
Leonard Sinclair

Louie, the Au Pair Syndrome and Other Tales
by
Leonard Sinclair

978-0-9567668-5-4

A copy of this book is deposited with the British Library

Published by

i2i Publishing. Manchester.
www.i2ipublishing.co.uk

Dedication:

To those I have had the privilege of meeting, treating and knowing over many years. I thank them for those lighter and most interesting moments.

Acknowledgements:

To my wife Ann for her help and criticisms
Arnold Levin for his generous support
Lionel Swift, Archie Sinclair and Joshua Sinclair

Photograph: Snowdon

About the Author

As an experienced consultant paediatrician and teacher, Leonard Sinclair has appreciated many diverse aspects of human nature in and beyond his work. His enjoyment of the quirks of human nature gives him great satisfaction. In these stories Leonard passes on some of the fascinating episodes which helped him to enjoy human relationships beyond that of the mere doctor - patient relationship.

Leonard has been a consultant paediatrician and biochemist on the staff of three major London teaching hospitals and visiting professor at several centres abroad. During the course of his career he has written several medical books and contributed to a medical encyclopaedia. He has also identified three genetic diseases but unlike others refuses to add his name to the titles.

He felt there is more to paediatrics than clinical and laboratory work. He hopes that these short stories illustrate a lighter side of practice and that it can sometimes be a less than happy experience to be behind the desk.

The stories are a mixture of humour, pathos and lessons to be learned. They represent incidents and situations that can occur to a medical man in and out of his professional art, at various stages of his development to become a consultant.

CONTENTS

Louie

She was young, about fifteen years old. The story was that she had gone to the toilet, and delivered the baby in the loo, into the lavatory pan. There was no wedding ring; she looked a little flushed, but was composed. A policeman had brought her to the hospital with her baby son, and now she was sitting up in bed in the open ward, wearing a cheap nightdress, and obviously new to this sort of thing. The baby was fine, that is apart from a prominent bright red raspberry coloured heart-shaped birthmark about two centimetres in diameter very evident on his left buttock.

The Ward Sister whispered the story to me. She did not know who the father was, but arrangements had already been made for the baby to be adopted. It seemed rather a mechanical approach, but what could one do about it in the circumstances? I asked the young mother if there were any problems. She said, there were none, but she did not know what name to call him.

A flash of inspiration came to me. "What about Louie?"

She nodded, but did not seem to see the point. Sister concealed a smile, and we moved on to the next patient. This was the first new born child that I had seen that year, that had been delivered into the toilet. She had successfully concealed her pregnancy, but from such uncertain beginnings, I wondered how she and her son would both get on later in life. When I saw the young mother a few days later, she seemed quite relieved and happy and was going home alone, and back to school.

Louie was picked up by an adoption society a few days later. Other than having a little diarrhoea and the birthmark, he seemed well, and quite a good-looking child at that.

In those days, an old friend had been quite generous to me and let me use his Consulting Room for private patients. They had been slow in coming, and I was struggling. I started writing a monograph whilst sitting there and waiting for patients to turn up. Since I had no receptionist I would take referrals by telephone by myself. One day the phone rang and a pleasant aristocratic voice asked whether he and his wife could make an appointment with me that afternoon for me to check a baby over for adoption.

I was pleased to do so at such short notice. They arrived an hour later, a charming couple who had not themselves been blessed with a child. They were adopting a baby, and I had been recommended to them as someone who might look him over before they actually made due application. He was feeding well and was quite a handsome child. There was nothing to find wrong with him, but when I turned him over, there was a heart-shaped red birth mark on his left buttock. I recognised Louie again. For one moment I thought he gave me a faint, knowing smile. I turned to the adoptive parents and said that he was a perfect child and that the birth mark would remain for some years, but would give him no trouble.

Louie was now five months old, and I thought that he had done rather well. I recounted the story to my wife when I got home, being quite happy that he had been well placed. She nodded in a vague sort of way when I explained it to her, but seemed to take it in.

Three months later while we were having breakfast she was reading through the birth columns in the morning paper. Suddenly she looked up and said,

"Do you remember Louie? Do you know that he is in the morning paper in the Birth Columns? He was christened in the font of a famous cathedral and that among his Godparents are distinguished members of the nobility and a high ranking member of the House of Lords." I smiled and finished my porridge. It occurred to me that the mother will never know, but I am sure she would have been very proud.

Some years later my wife accompanied me to a medical conference in a Northern city. Unusually, it was rather boring. There were dull speeches and uninteresting colleagues, so I returned to our hotel early and a little disaffected. My wife had meanwhile taken the opportunity to do a little shopping and came back all agog holding the local newspaper in her hand. It reported a disturbance in a shopping centre started by some boys from the local public school who were drunk. The names were recorded. One of them was Louie's new name. She reminded me of the story. I shrugged my shoulders. It all came back to me,

"So Louie has now become a Hooray Henry," I said. She smiled.

THE AU PAIR SYNDROME

The chief was in a bad mood. He had not received another merit award. As usual he let off steam in all directions. His favourite criticism was of the 'mediocrats,' the so-called 'creepies' who made professional progress without actually doing anything of significance except to say the right thing at the right time and in the right place. George, the registrar, regarded himself as an up and coming paediatrician. He was fed up with the moaning, but was somewhat relieved that the chief was soon off to play golf for the afternoon. He now had the unit to himself, and could get on with things possibly getting home early for a change, and keeping a theatre date in the evening.

It was much easier in the previous job. The chief was less heavy, more gentlemanly, distant, but always pleasant. George was thinking of this when the phone rang. By chance it was his previous boss and he needed George's help. He had booked a holiday, but the locum doctor who was to cover his work while he was away was ill and there was no-one to look after an outpatient clinic. He apologised for the short notice, but could George stand in for him that afternoon?

This was indeed short notice and the new chief would not like it. Still, there was some loyalty to his previous boss, and the already booked-in patients had to be considered. He agreed.

It was an arduous traffic laden journey through South London and George arrived late only to be scolded by the unpleasant outpatient sister. The patients were to George a dull and mundane lot. The screaming baby George easily recognised and diagnosed as having a fissure in ano. He explained this to a grateful mother, who had lost a great deal of sleep, as a crack in the anal canal that was stretched and its base opened up and exposed when a large motion or a great deal of wind was passed suddenly at night. He prescribed a local anaesthetic. The explanation took a long time, and sister kept on coming into the clinic to remind him that he was running late.

The last patient was unlike the others. She wore an expensive fur coat. She smelled of an expensive perfume and her daughter was well dressed. The complaint was 'stomach ache.' It had only begun a few weeks earlier and was getting worse. The general practitioner was not helpful, the mother stated. He had shrugged his shoulders and sent her child off for a second opinion. After questioning, George ascertained that the pain was in the left lower quadrant of the child's abdomen, and when he examined her he found tenderness as well as palpating a tightly contracted colon there.

He put it to the mother that her daughter had the irritable bowel syndrome. Mother did not understand this, but when George called it a spastic colon, she responded positively and wanted to know whether the cause could be psychosomatic because something had upset her daughter. It was getting late, but George felt that she needed more time. He agreed that it could be, and asked why she had brought this possible cause to his attention.

"Five weeks ago my husband got me and my daughter out of bed early in the morning, bundled us into the car and took us both to a small dirty looking house in one of the poorer parts of the district. He took us both in to this place, sat us down and told me that this was the place where my daughter and I were to stay in future. He was going to stay in the hotel where I had previously been living with him as his wife. It was his property and he did not want us to be with him there any longer. In any case he had grown fond of the au pair girl and she was going to be his partner in future. There was an argument and a fight and our daughter began crying. Since that time she has had this pain in her stomach."

George sat down and sat back. He felt that he had to listen to this distressed woman.

"We have been married for five years now and my husband has been repeatedly unfaithful. At first I did not mind. He is very immature and at one time I tolerated his behaviour, but now we have a daughter who is very upset, and I am pregnant again. What am I to do?"

George was sympathetic and offered some medicine, but as he began writing out the prescription she interrupted.

"This was not the first au pair girl that he got involved with. Last year I came home one evening and found him in bed with one. And there have been others. When we were staying with his mother he was chasing his mother's au pair round the flat one day. By the way doctor did you say that my daughter had a spastic colon? My husband's mother had the same condition. Can it be treated with colonic lavage?"

George nodded and said that some patients were treated in this way. Why did she ask?

"Well, I used to treat my mother-in-law with colonic lavage sometimes before we were married."

George was intrigued. "Why was that? Are you a nurse?"

"No, I was his mother's au pair girl"

By Any Other Name

This is the story of two men who differed in every way, and by circumstance achieved a certain amount of temporary fame. Their names which will be remembered for some time are recorded in different books, for different things, and are read for different reasons, by different people.

Let us begin with Hackenschmidt. Gerald Hackenschmidt's family were upper middle class. The parents were reasonably well off, and there were three sons. All were clever, different and argumentative. Their house was one of constant uproar and tension. Father would temporarily leave the home; mother was intermittently to be seen sobbing, and the three brothers were always in and out of the place. One became a famous photographer, the second one an engineer, and Gerald a doctor. When he was 17 he inherited a legacy with enough for him to be financially independent of his father. The allowance from the estate enabled him to leave home, live in a small flat in the city, and buy a sports car.

He always looked older than his years. He tended to talk through his nose, and wore gold-rimmed pince-nez. His speech had a lisp, which actually was not affected. There was always a superior manner about him. The idea of becoming a medical man attracted him, but he knew that with a name like Hackenschmidt, his chances of admission to one of the great halls of medical learning would be poor. He therefore engaged a solicitor, and changed his name by deed-poll to Hytten-Smith. Students of German will know that this is almost a literal translation. He was quite clever, but not brilliant. He managed to pass the appropriate examinations and was admitted to one of the older medical schools. There he affected a black jacket, striped trousers, spats and shiny shoes. He tended to associate with the wealthier students. Although he did not engage in the more physical sports such as rugby, he had a good handicap at golf, and was able to meet lecturers, professors and consultants on their own ground. Since he had a pleasant manner, he did well socially, although his academic progress was rather pedestrian.

There seemed to be some attraction between him and David Isaac who was short, dark with bushy eyebrows and a hooked roman nose. Isaac was muscular, alert, active, clever, and a good rugger player. He always answered questions directly. His speech may have been a little jumbled at times, but he was known to do well in the exams, and usually came top of the lists, winning several prizes. Socially, however, he tended not to mix, and did not go out of his way to pander to the Chiefs. He lived in lodgings in the east and poorer side of the city. He did not lunch with his fellows, and was often to be seen carrying his bread and cheese to the local park, afterwards hurrying off to the pub, to gulp down half a pint of beer in the lunch hour. He watched the pennies. He shined his own shoes. His cuffs were threadbare, his shirt collar did not quite fit, and he had an intense stare which was a little off-putting when he observed people. He always frowned when he listened. His trousers were baggy.

Hytten-Smith and Isaac occasionally met to speak about things, and there was a crude camaraderie between them in their infrequent associations. They would usually tell jokes to each other and they would make comments about lecturers and compare notes. Hytten-Smith was ready to seek advice and help from Isaac about subjects he could not understand. Isaac was always ready with explanations. Hytten-Smith would tell him about his weekend in the country with friends, but Isaac would be silent and most people knew that during those weekends after the Saturday game of rugger, he would be studying hard, or would go to the pathology museum, or be seen in the library. He was a hive of activity but he had not many friends, and was not socially attractive.

Their first meeting was an occasion when, one supposed, they sized each other up. It was on a coffee break in the medical school refectory. Two men with contrasting appearance and style found themselves sitting opposite each other. Gerald opened the conversation by asking David where he had his shirts made. David flushed.

"I buy my shirts in a shop. I do not know who makes them, probably some poor woman who is underpaid in a factory in the north. I wash my own shirts and iron them, I do everything for myself."

"Where did you go to school? Which public school were you at?" rejoined Gerald.

David thought that Gerald was trying to tease him and had a good answer.

"I went to one of the best public schools in Wales but if you are thinking that my father paid the fees you are quite wrong. I actually won a scholarship there. It was only by a piece of luck that I ever got there in the first place. I was never one of the privileged few. My father was a miner and I went to the local primary school. When I was ten years old the school held an examination to assess my progress because I was apparently not doing well at all. The Headmaster called me to his study to inform me that he was amazed at how well I had done in the terminal examination. He suggested that I would probably get an office job in the local mine. I had very different ideas from this and asked his permission to apply for the scholarship at the local public school.

"He seemed very amused and was rather hesitant that I should apply. Nevertheless, he let me go ahead, and on the appointed day I put on my best clothes and got the train to the school, took the examination and went for a very stiff interview. They asked me about my antecedents and my ambitions and I can tell you that I was sweating at the end of it, and felt that perhaps it was a waste of time."

Gerald was half-listening to this. Half his mind was on his latest conquest, a most pleasant fair-haired nurse in the orthopaedic ward. David was persistent however.

"It was quite interesting when I got the result of my examination. I was standing by the front door of the house where my mother was arguing with Mr James, the local butcher, about the price of the joint of meat that he had delivered. The postman pushed his way past Mr James and in his loud voice, announced, 'There is a letter, it looks an important one, for Mr David Isaac.' My mother was too preoccupied with arguing with the butcher to bother very much, and snatched it from him passing it over to me. I tore it open and to my delight found that I had won the scholarship. 'Mother,' I shouted, 'I have won the scholarship. Isn't that marvellous!' She was still arguing with Mr James and was so preoccupied that she absent-mindedly said, 'Very good, what does that mean?'

"I can tell you it was a struggle to keep me going there. There was a certain amount of snobbery and it was only because of my examination results that I got a place at this medical school, and also because I am quite a good rugger player. How did you manage to get a place here?"

Gerald made a depreciatory gesture, lowered his eyelids slightly and stared at the table.

"One has one's methods, you know, one has one's methods. There was not a great deal of difficulty."

This was the first time they had met and each gained something from the other's company. David had learned the methods of those who were advancing socially and Gerald had realised that he had quite a clever colleague.

Gerald used this more to his advantage than perhaps did David, and although he did not say so, David was a little flattered by the attentions of his posh friend.

There were other occasions when they met when their interest in each other widened and David was able to talk about his attitude towards the medical mores of the time and his sympathy towards the deprived and those in need. When Gerald tried to interest him in the world of art, music, theatre and even suggested a girlfriend most of Gerald's attempts were highly unsuccessful. David's attitude did not change. He was always critical of some of the consultants who arrived late for ward rounds after spending much of their time in their private practices, and was always worried when he knew the right answer to the questions on ward rounds. He was never asked very often and if he was, the insinuation was always made that he knew too much for his own good. There was apparently some lack of social graces and Gerald could never believe that David had passed the interview for admission to medical school. One day he taxed him about how he had gained entrance. David was fairly open about it,

"I applied to many medical schools and was not given an interview. But my father spoke to his manager at the mine, and the manager spoke to the owner of the pit. The owner's brother was actually the former Dean of this medical school, and he gave me a letter and the former Dean saw me especially on his own, and asked me all about my life and the mine and my scholarship, and he gave me a place. You can say it was by personal influence as I do not think I would have got here without my father's help and the generosity of the mine owner. Of course we have a new Dean now and I am not sure he is the same sort of man. He does not quite look me in the eye when he sees me in the quadrangle."

Gerald was amused by this trick of fate, but kept silent and looked interested. At that time he had taken up sailing and photography. His brother was good at the latter and was giving him advice. This was because he was heavily dating the daughter of the Senior Consultant Orthopaedic Surgeon in the hospital, and there was a prospect of a Mediterranean cruise. This could be quite enjoyable; it might have its tricky moments but there were obvious potential advantages. The work was not doing too badly and his engaging manner allowed him to seek advice from other students, in particular, David, who was warming towards him. They sometimes discussed how they might make progress in their careers. David was keen to take the Fellowship of the Royal College of Surgeons examination and become a surgeon. He had studied all the regulations for this postgraduate examination. He was trying to keep abreast of the advances in the subject; perhaps that is why he was thought to be a know-it-all. He was now teaching at Sunday school at the local chapel and earning a little from this and either because of economic circumstances or because he had been impressed by a vegetarian who had given him a lift when he hitchhiked home, he had stopped eating meat. He asked for a vegetarian meal and drank no wine at one of the final year dinners. One of the consultants questioned him closely about this. It was rather embarrassing, but David was firm in his conviction and the consultant was rather amused. As he put it, "A doctor should be a Bon Viveur."

David seemed rather a dull fellow and forceful in his arguments. He later confided his embarrassment to Gerald who warned him that the consultant concerned was a good friend of the new Dean and would probably be the next one. David shrugged his shoulders and walked off. They both passed their final medical examinations and Isaac qualified with honours.

Now the great bonus for a successful student was to be appointed to the House Staff as a Resident at that particular hospital where they had studied; to be a House Physician or House Surgeon, and to walk the wards with the chief. This was indeed an honour, and a good start to a medical career. Hytten-Smith's application was successful. The President of the golf club appointed him as his House Surgeon. Hytten-Smith realised that this would be an onerous job for him but he thought he could survive. David

Isaac had won the highest prizes and scholarships, but after all the appointments had been announced, he realised that he had not been appointed to a resident job at his own medical school. He had been left out. Everyone was surprised and he was furious. There was a saturnine flush about his face.

"It's no skin off my nose, I will go and see the Dean and give him a piece of my mind," was his comment. There was no point in cautioning him, it was better if he got it off his chest, and it did not matter to most of the other chaps anyway. They were safe.

He did see the Dean. In fact the Dean was a little evasive, and when David pressed the matter, the Dean said rather shamefacedly,

"Of course my boy, people of your race I am afraid, are not favoured in this hospital. I do wish it were otherwise, but that is how things are. Nevertheless, I will give you a good reference for another job. You never actually blotted your copybook here. I am sure you will get something elsewhere, and do well subsequently."

David reacted. "What about my race? I am very proud of being Welsh," he blurted out. The Dean looked puzzled and confused.

"Well, we thought you were a member of the Hebrew race," he muttered.

David was momentarily puzzled. At first he had no idea what was going through the Dean's mind, but when he quickly analysed the situation he realised that prejudice did not only extend to his people. He curtailed the conversation, stood up and bade farewell to a rather crestfallen Dean and made a dignified exit.

He decided to change his name to another on the advice of his friend Gerald Hytten-Smith with whom he discussed it in the pub that evening. Hytten-Smith did not actually let out the name of his own antecedents, but the advice was well taken, and David used his mother's maiden name and became David Rose.

In summary, although David had poor beginnings, he became a famous surgeon with a certain operation named after him. He was much in demand as a Lecturer, Teacher, Examiner, and developed a world-wide reputation. When he died his obituary took up two columns in the medical journals.

Of course, the medical journals and The Times and the quality newspapers did not devote any space to David's early humble origins and did not mention his failure to be recognised at his own medical school. In fact, he was only able to obtain a locum job at another hospital after many attempts at finding a more permanent position. Every time he applied and when his application form showed that he had been a brilliant scholar and student, those who were deciding about whether to appoint him looked rather astonished at a man with such a good academic record who had not been given a job in his own medical school. This was a stigma that he had to bear for many years but his keenness and skill had allowed him to pass the Fellowship examination and a sympathetic Chief of Staff at another London teaching hospital had enabled him to become a consultant there eventually. Once he had achieved this position the world was his oyster. He was happily married but never quite lost contact with his friend Gerald. Gerald would always write to him and they sent Christmas cards to each other and occasionally would meet in London.

Neither actually discussed their careers but their friendship grew and again Gerald would seek David's advice about surgical problems and David would ask about London life, the arts and music. By this time Gerald had found his level and had already made his mark in the legal world. He had been a failure as a House Surgeon, at his great teaching hospital, and was barely able to get another appointment. He did a few locum jobs in Lancashire, and in 1939 was called up to the army. He served in France, and after the German invasion luckily escaped back to Britain from Dunkirk. He arrived in England with very little left except his uniform, and after he reported for duty he was sent on indefinite leave and had very little with which to occupy himself.

On returning to his flat, he found a large batch of correspondence to be dealt with, including several claims from other members of the family, who thought he had received too much in his legacy. He was summoned to Court, and through not employing a Solicitor, lost his case. Being too proud to take legal advice he fought his case in the County Court and lost again. He took his case to the High Court and was again unsuccessful. However, he had more success in the Court of Appeal who dismissed his case, but allowed him to appeal to the House of Lords. He went to the House of Lords dressed in his uniform, and again affected a monocle. The whole process took a year and by this time he had learned a great deal about certain defined aspects of the law of inheritance, and indeed this time he won. His case was recorded amongst many others in the law journals and in most legal text-books. It is under the name of Hytten-Smith, and he has a small but important place in legal history. It is interesting to note that he was a doctor, not a lawyer but the particular piece of law he managed to change was quite complex and has stood the test of time.

Hytten-Smith then spent a difficult war in West Africa and ran foul of his commanding officer when involved with a recruitment campaign in Ashanti territory in Nigeria. He refused to allow some 'volunteers' to be recruited because of their poor state of health. He had found that they suffered from endemic malaria, and were quite unsuitable to join the army and even more unsuitable to be transported to Burma. He avoided a Court Marshall and travelled with his troops to India and took part in the campaign in Burma, being discharged from the Royal Army Medical Corps in 1946. He was thoroughly fed up and disconsolate when he discovered the report on his discharge papers questioned his character. Subsequently it took him 15 years to clear his name with the Ministry of Defence. He looked up David who gave him some sound advice. He was good at careers and was always helpful.

"You do not seem to be able to join a practice, no one seems to want you and it is very difficult to find practices now. Fortunately, I am in hospital medicine and I was quite lucky in the Air Force and got a lot of experience in surgery. Why don't you just put up your plate and since you are not that badly off, open a practice on your own somewhere where there seem to be no other doctors?"

Gerald toured south London and found a suitable spot. He bought a house, installing a housekeeper at the same time. The area where he worked was poor. The patients were dependent but he was always cheerful and ready to seek the advice of other doctors. He said that he learned most of his medicine this way. The practice grew and became so big that he took in other partners and became a senior practitioner. He took his time with his patients and did all his home visits himself. The waiting room in his surgery was crowded but the patients never complained because they knew he would spend time with them and was not only interested in their immediate medical condition.

He usually did well at Christmas with small presents from the population which he served, and was quite generous to those who were poverty stricken helping them to find housing and giving advice about work. At first, he went back to the societies in his old medical school and played a little golf but became increasingly busy and disinclined because the young men coming up in medicine seemed different from his crowd. His circle of friends diminished but he always had time for David Rose, his friends new name, who was very successful and the very few private surgical patients that he had, he would send to David who was prompt, courteous and skilful. There were moments of depression, and he often wondered if perhaps this phase of sobriety was not as happy as those earlier days when his attitude was less responsible.

A year before he died he met David at the latter's London club. They had dinner together and reflected on such sober thoughts. David was much more cheerful and looked back in perspective over their careers. He put it to Gerald that the work that they had both done had its own satisfaction, and it was quite probable that Gerald's was more valuable than his at the teaching hospital where he was a consultant. He was now a married man and had six children. He was also a lay preacher at his local chapel. He had wed a delightful Welsh lady and they were both determined that the children should be taught Welsh in Welsh at a Welsh school. He certainly was not going to send them to any public school when they grew up, and hoped that one of his boys might follow him in the profession.

Gerald was found dead in his bed one morning by his housekeeper. The news of Dr Gerald's death spread around the district very rapidly. There were many callers.

It seems a great shame that the obituary to David Rose did not actually mention his former name, that he had risen from humble origins, and the report of the High Court Case of Hytten-

Smith versus Golding on inheritance now recorded in legal text books as a standard piece of law, did not mention that it was really Hackenschmidt versus Goldschmidt, and that they were cousins.

As noted previously, Hytten-Smith and Rose were different men, they each had success in different ways, but the world dealt with them, not from the point of view of their contributions, abilities, or personalities, but mainly because, their new names sounded sweeter to the prejudiced ear.

Sammy's Dad

Charles was quite pleased with himself having passed the final Fellowship of the Royal College of Surgeons. It was his second attempt, and there had been a certain amount of luck, but one always discounted this when successful. The FRCS had been simple by comparison to the Driving Test which he had failed miserably on six occasions. If it had not been for Sammy he would never have got the licence. Sammy had been very kind, and had taken him out for a whole day, instilled confidence in him, and explained to him most of the manoeuvres. Afterwards, Charles took Sammy out for a drink to show his gratitude. When they parted Sammy said,

"Remember you owe me one."

This was no false prediction. A week later he was on the phone. This was on a Sunday morning. It was about his elderly father, old Sammy. Would Charles come around? The old man had just been in hospital to have his prostate removed. The man who was discharged was not the same man as the one who had gone into hospital. He was incontinent of urine and seemed confused. He spent most of the time staring into the distance, could not move around, and when he had tried to get out of bed, he had fallen on the floor. Sammy had called an emergency doctor, who suggested that they would not be able to manage him and that the old man should go into a home. It was also suggested that he had suffered some brain damage. This had alarmed his wife. She called Sammy. He tried to communicate with his father, but could not do so. Sammy was anxious for another opinion, and so called his friend Charles who could not refuse to come.

One supposes that after passing an exam one feels that the world is one's oyster, and full of confidence Charles put all of his newly-bought instruments into a case, and toddled off to Sammy's father's place. It was in Shepherd's Bush, overlooking Shepherd's Bush Green. In the 1950s it was a relatively pleasant area.

There was no lift and he had to climb four flights of stairs. He was very surprised when he got to the flat that it had a marble floor. The old man was sitting bent over the kitchen table. He was pale, and looked into the distance with rather a blank stare. He still had some white hair, and thin black eyebrows. His eyes were partially hooded, his face lacked expression, and he was drooling at the mouth. Charles tried to engage him in conversation, but there was no reply. He tried telling a few jokes, but there was no response. Sammy explained that the old man had been like this for two or three days. The room smelled of urine, and it looked as if the emergency doctor's diagnosis may have been right.

It was suggested that the old man be moved to his bedroom, put on the bed, and undressed, so that Charles might examine him. This was a difficult task. The old man virtually had to be dragged across the marble floor, and half carried into his bedroom. When he was in the bed, Sammy undressed him. Charles's examination was very detailed. The abdomen was easily palpable, but there was a very full bladder there, and when he touched it, urine was passed into the bed, this to everyone's embarrassment.

There were also signs that the brain had received some damage. The blood pressure was very high, there was a murmur in the heart, and it was obvious the old man had early cataracts. Charles was not sure whether he had just had a stroke or not, but all in all it was evident that the emergency doctor's diagnosis was fairly close to the mark, and Charles began to think that his own intervention had been unseemly and untimely. What could he do?

He covered Sammy's father up, and looked around. Sammy was standing in the large bay window of the flat, looking out over Shepherd's Bush Green, and Charles slowly walked over to his friend, meanwhile desperately trying to think of something to say. When he got to Sammy, just as he was going to speak to him, he heard a faint noise behind. It was the old man calling to his son. The voice was rather, croaking and low-pitched.

"Sammy, Sammy, come … over …" The power of speech seemed to be fading from the old man. Both men rushed over to the bed. The old man looked very bad at this point. Sammy put his ear close to his father's mouth, and Charles leaned forward to hear what appeared to be the old man's last words.

"What is it, daddy?" Sammy said. The old man made a tremendous effort, saliva drooled from his mouth. He turned his face towards his son, and seemed to catch his eye. His head fell back, his breathing was laboured. He was making this tremendous effort to say something. He just about made it, and Charles leaned forward again desperately trying to hear. The old man sighed, he turned his head towards Sammy again, his face was twisted, and almost in a murmur, he spoke.

"Don't pay him more than five guineas," he said. Sammy looked up at Charles and smiled,

"Well, you seem to have cured him."

The old man actually got better within a few weeks and lived another five years. Charles remembered the story for years to come. It kept him in order.

Uncle Raphey's Clock

When I was a child I was rather afraid of him. He used to talk to himself. To this day I have never been able to understand the phenomenon. I call it auto-communication but when Raphey did this he would shake his body as well. Later on I realised that in fact he was sometimes, just saying his prayers and he would mutter them to himself. He was a religious man, but I knew that when he prayed instead of putting his hands together he would wave them around, and hold his arms aloft rather like Elijah as he looked up to Heaven. He was not insane, quite normal at the best of times, and when I grew older I realised that he was a mild, quiet and inoffensive, gentle, sweet person. He never did any work, but he pressed his trousers every day and sometimes, when I was visiting my great grandfather's house, I used to watch him do this. He never married. I did not know why he took such care of his appearance. Everyone in the family accepted Raphey as he was, except Polly, the housekeeper, who was afraid of him, and would never stay in the same room alone with him.

There are always stories about people like Raphey. He did not communicate much and never even referred to it, but he had been in the so-called Great War, and of all things he had been in the South Wales Borderers. Fancy that. They said that he had starved in the trenches because he told the authorities that he was a vegetarian. Indeed, when he came home from the war he was like a skeleton. This exaggerated his thin cadaverous face, but later he developed a paunch. All the other uncles spoke about the heroics and difficult times in the trenches, but when they sounded off he seemed to take no interest in the subject and would wander away out of sight

As part of his bachelor life, he would occasionally take me out as a young companion to the music halls for a pleasant evening and later he treated me, on occasions, to a Gilbert & Sullivan opera. He always took a taxi and hardly spoke to me when we went, but I enjoyed the evenings and felt quite relaxed with him, although it was a little embarrassing to see him talking to himself in the middle of a theatrical performance.

The rest of the time he busied himself about the house, dusting, cleaning and checking up on Polly. He always rose in the mornings about 6 o'clock to say his prayers. He made his own breakfast before anybody else was up and then went on a constitutional. When his father died he inherited the remnants of an antique business. He looked after his unmarried sister at home, and tended her, mainly by himself, with the district nurse when she was dying and stayed on his own in their small flat after this.

I would dutifully pay him a visit once every few weeks, and have a chat with him. I felt I should do this, although he never seemed lonely or to need company and appeared to be quite content with his simple life. We would sit each side of the fireplace. Between us was his prize possession, a beautiful antique mantel clock. It stood on the mantelpiece and was some two feet high. It was made of white Italian marble. The hands were gold, the dial surmounted an arch under which was the pendulum, a swing with a golden little boy sitting on it. It was quite beautiful. It needed some adjustment every day, and the stand had to be balanced. The clock was protected by a glass dome about three feet high. This was something that Raphey valued greatly. Apart from his prayers and the strange way he would undertake them, the clock seemed to be very important to him. Sometimes as I was having a cup of tea with him he would suddenly get up and clean the glass dome. When he did this he seemed to be preoccupied, oblivious of the fact that I was watching him.

As a child I wondered if his prayers might ever be answered. He certainly seemed to have survived the war, and had lived longer than his younger sister, but he had a cloistered life, apparently no friends and as he grew older, he rarely went out except to do a little shopping. Apart from me and a few relatives he had not many visitors. He seemed to be more interested in things than in people. I knew that he prayed three times daily and was intrigued about his spirituality. There was certainly something strange about him, and above all it seemed to me that the clock was something of an idol.

I had some holiday and nowhere to go, so that one morning I thought I would pop in to see him. I found him surprisingly disconsolate. I soon found out why. He had moved the clock to clean it and the glass cover had fallen on the floor and was smashed and he told me that the clock would not function unless it was in the glass case. I was amazed to see a man so upset about it but told him that I would try to find another glass case.

Taking the measurements with me I made a trip to Brighton and searched all the second hand shops in the Lanes for a replacement, found one that I thought would be suitable and after some haggling, bought it. I took it to him the next day. It fitted perfectly. He was almost in tears and blessed me. He said that he would leave the clock to me after he had died. He knew I would look after it properly He had not made a will, but I was to remember that the clock was to be mine. This was my inheritance from him.

The only time he actually telephoned, was for medical advice. He had had trouble passing water and had consulted a well-known surgeon who had suggested an operation. He was apprehensive and reluctant to have surgery, and had put things off. My mother told me in confidence that he was already making arrangements for his own funeral and had bought his tombstone. This was a strange idea and part of the cult of the elderly in the 1930s and 1940s. Raphey regarded entrance to a hospital as a possible exit from this world. I went down to his flat and persuaded him that he should have the operation since the surgeon was an eminent man. Reluctantly, he agreed, but asked me to take him to the hospital myself and stay with him there for a little while. I took the morning off and picked him up. He was very nervous, frail and tremulous. He opened up a little on the way and said he was more afraid of being in hospital than he was of the Germans in the Great War. At least he could see the Germans, but he could not understand what was wrong inside his body. When we arrived I took him to his room, settled him down, leaving some fruit and flowers for him.

After a few minutes I thought I would pop back and take another look. I found he was praying again and shaking his body, with his head bent forwards as if he were facing Heaven. I smiled at this because I was used to his strange habits, but as I walked away, I had a sense of foreboding and was a little apprehensive.

He had the operation the next day and recovered from the anaesthetic. I visited him several times and all seemed well although he was still anxious. I was able to reassure him but he nodded dumbly as I spoke to him and as I tried to leave his room he would call me back and say,

"Do remember, when I go, you can have the clock." This left me with some sense of foreboding.

I was called in the early hours of one morning a week later to be told that Raphey had suddenly collapsed and died. There was no one else in town, so I made my way to the hospital. As I entered his room I noticed that he was uncovered. I saw his grey cadaverous face, the mouth flopped open: it was as if he were still alive. His arms were outstretched; the elbows bent his hands unclasped. It was a strange posture. He was desperately pale. Obviously he had bled.

As I looked at him there was a rustling behind me and the resident doctor appeared. I knew about him and had met him a few days before. He was a brilliant dental student and was taking a medical degree to complete his training. He would return and one day he would be a leader in his profession. His name was Cyril Forth. The boys all called him Sea Forth because he was a Highlander and was a high flyer as well. Now he was crestfallen and looked worried.

He confessed that he knew that Raphey had bled to death but that he could not find a vein, and could not get the blood transfusion going in time. There had been no one else available at the time to help him. He was pale, worried and apprehensive. He asked me not to report him to his chief because the Ward Sister had not been able to find him quickly enough and he said he was very sorry. After all, Raphey was an old man anyway. I suppressed my momentary anger because of his anguish. All sorts of nasty thoughts came into my mind, but I held them back and in as dignified a manner as possible asked him if he would leave me alone with my uncle. I arranged for the body to be covered and said prayers. He would have liked this. He was fond of his prayers.

There was the usual telephoning to other relatives and it was not until a week later and after the funeral that I remembered the clock. I thought I would pop down to Raphey's flat to see what had happened to it. When I got there nothing had been changed. I found a few old books that obviously he had read and some photographs in a cupboard behind the door. When I looked at the mantelpiece the clock had gone. I had been more upset and worried about my uncle's untimely death than about possessions but it seemed very strange that my inheritance had vanished. It must have been quite valuable at the time, but this did not concern me. It would have been a nice remembrance of the old man but it was obviously not to be. By some strange power it had disappeared.

I always remembered Raphey and said prayers by his grave when visiting those of my other relations. Of course, on reflection I realised that young Dr Forth had been quite friendly with the old man, and they had seemed to hit it off when Raphey had come into hospital first of all. Indeed, after the operation Raphey had told me that he liked the fellow. Nevertheless, every time I visited the grave, I remembered the unfortunate circumstance of his death.

I had some contact with dentists and at one time lectured to them on medical matters. I did this in collaboration with the man who later became my friend. We were very successful with our examination results. We did some research together and we hit it off well. Everything we did together was successful. There are some relationships like this, and I valued his collaboration and friendship, but we lost contact over a period of years, and whilst I plodded on with my career he rose to the heights of being a Dean at one of the major dental schools.

Time passed. My son had never really wanted to be a doctor and although he had places offered, he could never quite achieve the academic demands in Physics required by the university. On his second attempt he decided that he would like to be a dentist. By the time he had his results and had made this decision, most of the places had been given to others. He rang around the dental schools in London, and was told that there were two vacant places at one of those better-known. I did not fancy his chances because although he was practical, sensible and gifted, his academic standards at examinations were not high. I was much against using influence to help the young, but felt that he was quite sincere in his purpose. I had seen personal influence used so frequently, nevertheless I decided to ring my dental friend of old since he was now a dean, to consult him and get his advice. When I telephoned he recognised my voice immediately and over the line it was evident there was still a certain bond between us. I asked if I might collar him early the next morning, and he readily agreed to see me then, offering the usual cup of tea when I came. I sat down in his office, and he immediately asked me how my son was getting on.

"He must be thinking about going to university by now, I would say," he said.

"Yes, Ron, that is perfectly true, so you probably know why I have come here." He smiled.

"Well, I can tell you now that I have no places in this dental school at all. One of my own professor's sons has just been refused a place already, and he has high academic attainments. I am afraid I cannot help you." I knew this already but it was clear in my mind what I wanted of him.

"Oh, no, Ron, he is a good boy and will make a very fine dentist, and will not let anyone down, but there is a place at another dental school (I mentioned the name) and I wondered if perhaps you know anything about it." Ron smiled.

"Yes, of course I know about it. Cyril Forth is the Dean there. We call him 'Sea Forth' because he is a Highlander and he was a high flyer when he was young. You know he has a medical degree as well, and he is a particular friend of mine. I am going to ring him as soon as you go and recommend your son for a place. I will tell him I have known him since he was a baby and he owes me one."

As he mentioned Cyril Forth's name a cold shiver ran down my spine. A momentary vision of my uncle Raphey lying in bed in his posture of prayer came to me. I must have temporarily been unaware of what Ron was saying.

"Are you alright, old boy?" he said. I came round and smiled at him but said,

"Oh, yes. I was just thinking about things and I am very grateful to you."

My son went for an interview a few days later and was fortunate to gain a place at dental school. He is now a qualified dental surgeon. He was interviewed by Cyril Forth. The date of the interview and the day of the week was the same as that when Uncle Raphey had died many years before. At the interview the Dean told my son that he felt a little strange but he offered him a place.

We never found the clock.

Broken Silence

Francois always looked a rather strange lad to me. I remember having tea with him and Jean and Marie, his parents, many years ago, when he would intermittently look into the distance, whilst you were talking to him. He had that glassy stare and always seemed to be in a rather dreamy state. He doodled some strange pictures and diagrams. Everything looked as if it was drawn in a mirror, and it was obvious that he was fantasizing most of the time. He was pleasant enough and agreeable, but the parents had wrapped him in cotton wool and handled him with kid gloves. He had always been spoiled. He came to England to study languages, and initially had done well, but subsequently failed most of his exams. His parents gave him an enormous allowance. He had managed to crash three cars, and had strange relationships with his girlfriends. He ran after them a great deal, but no young lady seemed attracted to him. He had a flat in South West London, and kept himself very much to himself. I occasionally saw him wandering around the streets in central London. He seemed aimless in his activities. When greeted he seemed to know me, but I was never quite sure. The one luxury that he had was to be psychoanalyzed. He felt that this would give him a healthier mind. It was a fashionable and expensive hobby, and one was not sure how much good it did him and whether he actually needed it or not.

When his parents came to London to do their shopping, they stayed in a very luxurious mansion. They often invited us out to dinner at restaurants we could not afford. Occasionally Francois came along. He was always uncommunicative, and did not join in our animated and sometimes witty conversations. It took a long time for him to give his order to the waiter, but his parents always waited patiently for him to do so. He was no trouble, and they seemed to accept him as he was, although I gather he was often heavily in debt.

So I was not surprised one morning to have an urgent telephone call from the parents. They were on holiday in Switzerland. They had had no contact with Francois for two weeks. He had not telephoned them, and there was no reply from his flat. This was unusual since he often rang them asking for more money. They asked whether, perhaps, I would go around and find him. He was not in his flat, and the caretaker had not seen him for at least a week. He told me that the lady next door was friendly with Francois and perhaps she would know something about him. I knocked on the door, and was readily admitted. She actually had the key of his flat, and said she had not seen him for some time, but he often popped in. She would not admit me to his flat at all, because she had not really got his permission, but she understood the problem. The only suggestion that she had as to where he might be was with his psychoanalyst. She gave me his address and telephone number.

When I returned home, I telephoned this gentleman, whom I knew vaguely professionally, and asked whether he knew Francois' whereabouts. His reply was abrupt.

"He is staying with me at my house at the moment."

I said that I was rather surprised at this, because professionally this was most unusual. The excuse was that Francois was now very ill, and needed intensive psychoanalysis. I demurred and said that perhaps he ought to be in hospital or a nursing home.

"You have no right to tell me how to run my practice," was the reply. I put it to him that this was not professionally correct. I found myself in a difficult situation and asked whether I could speak to Francois over the telephone, and was told that he was in no mood to speak to me.

I immediately telephoned his parents, and advised them to come to London.

They arrived the next day. I met them at the airport, and explained the difficulties over professional ethics. We were able to enter Francois' flat. It stank of Gaullois tobacco. It was otherwise sparse. We imagined that he had been selling furniture for money, since despite his large allowance he was rather prodigal. I nosed around, and was fortunate enough to find his National Health number and card. Even more fortunately I found that his General Practitioner was a friend of mine. His practice was a short distance away, and I walked around to see him. He greeted me like an old friend and offered me a cup of coffee. He was not doing anything at the time, and I explained the situation to him in full.

"There is no problem," he said. "He is a patient of mine, I can ring this psychiatrist fellow, and ask that we either have a second opinion, or that he be released to his parent's house." He did this. The telephone call took a long time, but we understood that the agreement was that another psychiatrist might see Francois. Arrangements were made that day, the second psychiatrist saw Francois, and Francois was able to be let out to stay at his parents' mansion.

I thought I had done my duty by my friends, but I telephoned a few days later to see how things were getting on. They pressed me to go around and see them, because they had further problems. When I arrived they were both sitting downstairs looking very glum. They had a problem. Francois was inert; he would not talk. Apparently he had been like this for the previous two weeks. He was upstairs in his room, and was uncommunicative. The psychiatrist who had seen him wanted to admit him compulsorily to a psychiatric Unit, but the parents would have preferred him to be a voluntary patient. Since he could not or would not speak to them, they could not gain his permission, and they wondered whether I might not be able to do something about it.

I went upstairs, knocked on the door of his room. There was no reply, so I knocked again. I pushed open the door; the smell of Gaullois cigarettes greeted me. It was pungent, and there was blue haze in the dark room. I made out the figure of Francois sitting with his back to me in a strange posture. His arms were akimbo, his legs were sprawled out in front of him, and there was no expression on his face. There was a small stub of a cigarette behind his right forefinger and second finger; the ash had burned down so that it was touching his flesh. He seemed unaware that his fingers were burnt. I sat down near him, and called his name. Needless to say there was no reply. I then thought that I would challenge him, because it struck me at the time that if he was able to light his cigarettes there must be some activity in his mind, and that he was probably partially aware of his surroundings.

"Francois, how are you?" There was no reply. "Francois, I have come to see you. Do you remember me?" Still no reply. "Francois, I am sorry to bother you, but your parents are rather worried about you, as I am, and we want to help, will you not speak to me at all?" It was as if I was speaking to a wall. He gazed into the distance. He was entirely mute.

"Francois, really, this is very rude of you. I have come here as a friend. You have known me for some time, and you are not being at all helpful, Francois." I noticed a faint flicker of interest in his face, but he was again unresponsive.

"Francois, you know your parents are very worried, your sisters have spoken to me, we have had a special doctor to you, and unless you can sign papers he will take you to a psychiatric unit compulsorily, and you will be there for some time." Francois moved slightly but seemed uninterested.

I knew at this point that he could understand something of what I was saying. I realised that although he had schizophrenia, there was some element of communication. I had always felt that he had been rather spoilt by his parents, but I had never told them this, so that I felt that the time had now come to be aggressive.

"Francois, you are a spoiled brat. You have always had your own way. You spend all your parents' money. You have never had a job. This is how you enjoy life. You have never contributed to society. Quite honestly, Francois, you disgust me! Francois, I think the best thing for you is to go to the fruit farm. You know what that is, it is a lunatic asylum. You will not have your own flat; you will not be able to go out and crash a car. You will be confined to a ward with other mental patients who are bizarre. You will occasionally be allowed to have a bath. The food will be awful and if you do not eat you will be forcibly fed, and if you misbehave you will be confined in isolation, possibly a strait-jacket!" Francois' eyes flickered slightly.

"Francois, I know you can understand what I am saying. I am not going to plead with you any longer; I am telling you quite frankly that I am personally fed up with you. I have watched you over the years, and I could never understand your behaviour, but what I am telling you now is that you have a choice. You can either sign a form and go as a voluntary patient to a respectable psychiatric unit where you will be well looked-after or you will be sectioned. In other words, you will being taken off by two male nurses and physically manhandled; taken by an ambulance, possibly forcibly restrained and given drugs to keep you quiet. Then you will be taken to another unit which will be most unpleasant. You have the choice, Francois, and I do not really care what happens to you, because as I have said before, I have always felt that you have not lived up to your parents expectations. You have not been a reasonable member of society, and quite frankly I am beginning not to like you at all. Other people have tolerated you but I do not know whether they really feel that you are a good person, because you are so insolent and useless, and have caused a lot of trouble to people unnecessarily. As for this luxury of having psychoanalysis it has been a waste of time. Why? A waste of money and really you ought to be ashamed of yourself. I am personally fed up with you."

Francois's face suddenly became contorted and went red. He drew up his legs, but did not say a word. I went on.

"Francois, you really make me sick. You had an opportunity for an education, and you wasted your time. You are playing up like an infant. You did well up to a point, but now you are impossible. If I had been your parents many years ago I would have got rid of you as a person who was inadequate for society. Personally, I would have been ashamed of you. You are a useless human being, and I do not know why I am wasting my time talking to you at all, but I warn you that I shall speak to the psychiatrist, and suggest that you are forcibly removed from here, that you go from the luxury of this home to a Mental Hospital, and there you will remain for a few years. It will not be pleasant. We call this the 'fruit-farm.' We will say that you are rather fruity, and people will occasionally be able to visit you. I wish you luck, you make me fed up, Francois."

Francois suddenly turned on me. His face contorted again. The posture of his limbs returned to normal. He dropped the stub of his cigarette on to the carpet. His mouth twisted,

"Piss off!" he said. "Piss off," he hissed at me.

"Well, I am pleased you did speak at last, Francois. It proves to me that you can say something."

I had had enough, but I knew he could speak, and I knew he was responsive. I knew that he could sign the appropriate papers and that I had broken through his façade.

I left his room and slowly descended the stairs to see his anxious parents. They were standing at the bottom of the stairs together looking very depressed. They looked up when they saw me, and rather plaintively and in unison they said to me,

"Did he say anything?"

"Yes," I said.

"What did he say?" I considered the matter for the moment and said,

"Yes, he did say a few words."

"What exactly did he say?" they repeated.

"Well, his exact words were, 'Piss off!' I said. They threw up their hands in joy. They were delighted by this. I had seemed to break through to this young man in my rather bullying, aggressive approach. He agreed to go, went as a voluntary patient, and actually responded to treatment.

His parents, and my wife and I often dined out, but we never mentioned this again, although I thought I would write the story some time.

The Knipple

When picking up odd words of Yiddish in my youth, I often wondered what a knipple was. Now I know that it is really a bride's dowry, but the word was misused in our family. We inferred that it was a stash of gold. In this case it was put away in a 'beitel' or strong leather purse. There always seemed to be something illegal, with a whispering quality, somewhat unsavoury about the word but it merely means money saved up and often hidden away.

As you know, treasures are found all over the world and dug up sometimes in pots, sometimes in boxes and sometimes scattered about and discovered in the soil. There must be many of these hoards of different types throughout the world, but they are always of interest. The one that I am most interested in involves one hundred gold sovereigns that were hidden for sixty four years and events that began in Poland, at the beginning of the twentieth century, and just before the First World War and onwards for more than half a century.

After her father had died, my grandmother, fearing an arranged marriage not of her choice, set up by her oldest brother, had eloped with my grandfather who was quite an attractive man. He was also was quite adept at smuggling himself and his bride out of Poland and travelling to other countries. By the time he was twenty, he had travelled to the United States, France, to the Low Countries and to England where he brought his newly-wed wife. As you can imagine, when they came to London at first, the family lived in rather deprived circumstances.

I never saw my grandmother's youngest brother, Lev, my great uncle, but from descriptions given by others he seemed to be a small, well-featured man with an alert face and brushed-back black hair. Lev had been left behind in Poland by his sister, had an uncomfortable time with his older brother, but found it more difficult to leave that country. However, his brother-in-law, my grandfather, obtained a forged Austrian passport for him. Lev crossed the border and got to Vienna, and eventually to the Adriatic, and travelling on a tramp steamer, came to England. He was met at the docks by my grandfather who seemed to know the part of the underworld that transmitted escapees from the oppression in the East to the slums of the West. Lev lived with my grandparents obtained work and was quite a successful man. I am not sure what he did, but he was certainly a hard worker. He enjoyed life and young ladies were apparently very fond of him. He paid for his keep, but was unaware of banks and put all his money away in a leather purse which he hid under his mattress.

By early 1914 it was evident that there would be a war. My grandfather had smelled this and he was worried about his brother-in-law's forged Austrian passport. He suggested that for a small sum Lev could be transported to the New World, and that one of his friends would smuggle him across the Atlantic to Canada and a new life there. There was some heart-searching about this for both of them, but at the time there were bad feelings about foreign nationals and potential enemies in this country. So Lev agreed. He was smuggled on a steamer to Toronto and settled in a small town just outside. Some say he had every intention of returning after the war. He never did. Others suggested that he had left behind personal problems in England. Certainly there were many visitations from young ladies to my grandparent's house after he had departed. He must have intended to come back, because he left one hundred golden sovereigns in the leather bag for my grand-parents to keep and look after for him so that he might have something, were he to return to this country. But he never did and the money stayed here in the beitel.

Far from it being the Golden West, life in Canada was very hard. He found it difficult to make his way as an illegal immigrant but eventually was able to make some sort of living. He did write a letter to my mother every month.

She would reply and would always give a good account to the family of his progress, his difficulties and how life was treating him. He never mentioned the sovereigns.

From this correspondence it was evident that after five years he was unlikely to return. The knipple now resided inside the mattress of my grandparent's bed. Only they knew about it. Lev wrote about a young lady he had met and intended to marry. She did not know this yet, and he was saving up to buy her an engagement ring. After a few years he was married and settled down, having both a son and a daughter. Life in Canada was becoming easier. Again, he never once wrote to ask about the sovereigns.

By 1931, when England went off the gold standard, his brother-in-law, my grandfather, never exchanged his hard-earned sovereigns for paper money. He now kept them and hid them under the floorboards in his small warehouse. This was because one night he found his younger son examining the bulge in his bed that now appeared on the surface of the mattress.

Actually, both of Lev's children did well. One became an accountant and the other a rather gracious and lovely person who worked hard and was popular in her husband's shop. She had married a delightful man and would write to my mother about her clever son. She was comfortable but not really wealthy so that every year they would promise to come over and we would promise to go to Canada. But for many years we never did.

During the Second World War a host of servicemen who were all sent by Lev from Canada, visited my parents and grandparents and were entertained by them. He did write, but now infrequently. He also sent his photograph. He was no longer a sprightly thing. He was now old and thin and was a minute figure in the foreground with Niagara Falls in the background. He never mentioned the money.

During the Second World War bombs rained down on London and indeed one fell on the warehouse. I never knew at this stage that the knipple was moved back to my grandmother's pillow and wrapped up in three pillow cases. It must have been very uncomfortable to sleep on and was carried ritually every night to the communal air raid shelter. After grandfather died we discussed many things about the family and Lev and the early life in Poland, the struggles and successes. The knipple was never mentioned. And indeed I would not have heard about it had it not been for a chance conversation with my cousin, Lev's grandchild.

He was now a successful doctor. His mother, Lev's daughter, had suffered a serious illness. When she recovered from that and major cardiac surgery, she decided to have a holiday in England, partly to convalesce. The costs of her illness had been immense and their savings had melted away. In 1978 she and her husband came to London on a package holiday, to a family function. We were all so delighted to see her. She carried herself with a certain grace, charm and pleasantness, and she seemed so happy to be with us.

We would take her out most days, but one afternoon she and her husband disappeared and at the time we did not know what had actually happened. Later I learnt that she visited my mother and her brother for tea, and my mother presented her with a beautiful tea set, and also gave her the inheritance from her father, Lev. The brown leather sack still contained the 100 sovereigns. The bag had a string around it and had spent some time in a pillow case having been missed by burglars, and life had become too dangerous for her to hold on to them; anyway it seemed only fair to give Sarah her inheritance. They both cried. Those glittering coins had lain dormant and unnoticed for sixty four years. Lev had passed away many years before, but his little hoard was put to good purpose. The sovereigns were spent on a good holiday not long before Sarah passed away.

It is a law that if you are given something valuable to look after for someone else, you must guard it more than if it were your own. My family knew this.

THE GIRL WITH RED HAIR

I never knew whether it had been a good thing for me to have taken the degree in Biochemistry in the middle of my medical course. I had been told it would have long-term advantages. I suppose it was useful to have a few more letters after my name, but it had been something of a sacrifice for my parents who were supporting me at the time. I had done quite well after I had taken my Medical Finals, but I was not favoured at my teaching hospital for one of the esteemed house jobs which are such a useful opening to a medical career. The favoured few did not seem to me such an outstanding lot. Those who commiserated with me told me that I had been extremely unfortunate. I needed a good reference to get another job, and was not prepared to argue.

It was generally rumoured that to obtain such an appointment one needed influence. I had only my own ability and knew that some of those who had been successful and whose parents were doctors had actually told me that father had referred private patients to the consultants. I knew that some of them had met the chiefs at medical meetings and certainly at social events. My lack of success was partly my own fault because I had been more than openly frank with the consultant who was chairman of the Selection Committee several months before. She was an interesting lady, and in some ways a courageous person; she was also rather outspoken and could be tetchy at times.

The incident occurred during one of her clinics. Nurse had disappeared for an unusually long time and had not called the next patient into the clinic. Our lady consultant stamped her feet and complained openly to us about the nurse, who was probably helping a handicapped man to the lift. Because of the delay, she then asked whether one of us students would go out and call in the next patient. One of our number was a Nigerian. He was a quiet and somewhat dignified young man who later on spent many years working in a Missionary Hospital in his own country. He was nearest the door. He got up immediately almost as if in response to a command, and hurried out. To our surprise the consultant seemed upset by this. On reflection now I realise that she must have been of a somewhat nervous disposition. She stamped her foot again, turned and glared at the student body and said,

"Never let a man like that attend one of my patients or call one of my patients in again. I know we live in a tolerant and liberal society but there are limits." She looked towards us for acknowledgement but was greeting with stony silence. Peter, who was standing next to me, and whose father had been a Professor in

Czechoslovakia and was a refugee in this country, could not forbear to respond to this by demurring and saying,

"I hope you will not hold it against him too much, Ma'am." She scowled at Peter and, looking at me – at the time one of her favourites – said,

"He is lucky enough himself to be in this country, isn't he?" There were rumblings in the back row, and obvious dissent amongst the student body. I got up to speak just as our Nigerian friend was returning with the next patient and tried to hold him back. The consultant was not satisfied by this.

"Are you afraid to support me?"

"No, Ma'am," I retorted, "but when you said that, you hurt me because both of the said gentlemen are friends of mine. However, I do agree with you whole heartedly that we live in a tolerant and liberal country." My colleagues clapped and roared approval and we all left the clinic together. From that day on I was a marked man, and my more socially adaptive friends warned me that this lady consultant was making scathing remarks about tactless students on ward rounds.

It turned out that the lady chaired the Selection Committee for resident appointments several months later, and I, of course, was unsuccessful. At this time I was very upset and disappointed, I walked all the way home to my lodgings. On the way I found myself following one of the Professors. I hurried on after him and caught him up to join him. He had always seemed to be a sympathetic man, and in the heat of the moment I unburdened myself. To my surprise he seemed to know about my predicament. He was kind and pleasant but gently told me that there was a time and place to say things and as a medical man I should know that tact and diplomacy were important in dealing with certain people. I was not perhaps as receptive as I might have been in the circumstances, and certainly did not react, holding my anger inwardly. It was a long walk to the digs. I made myself something to eat when I got there, went to bed and got up at 11 o'clock the next morning. There was something of a feeling of relief. I had been apprehensive and now it was all over. There was nothing to do. I was free, there were no lectures, no ward rounds, no more studying… for a spell at least. I was now a qualified doctor but had no job and my prospects were not as good as they might have been.

I made several unsuccessful applications for resident hospital appointments and was not even called for interview, but after a few weeks, I was fortunate enough to be appointed as a House Surgeon to a small district general hospital on the

East Coast. I spent some 15 months there. The work was sometimes exhausting but the spirit of the place was directed to the patients, and although I enjoyed my tennis, the parties, the occasional drink in the local pub, much of the emphasis was put on medical skill. There was a friendly rivalry over making the correct diagnosis and assessing the patient right. The junior doctors shared their knowledge and skills. Most of them were older than I and several came from the Commonwealth. I think I was still a little outspoken, but we were so busy it did not seem to matter to some of them, who were even more outspoken.

I then had to think about my future and considered going into general practice. After all, I had not been favoured at my own teaching hospital and at the time this would be a mark against my becoming a consultant. I felt it would be useful to get a job in paediatrics – treating children's diseases and improve upon my general training and so become a more complete family practitioner. I applied for ten jobs and was unsuccessful in all my applications. There was intense competition. However, I was very surprised to be offered an interview at the Children's Hospital, where I myself had been a patient at the age of seven years. On reflection, my stay there as a child had not been entirely pleasant, but this was the only prospect I had for work, and I certainly grasped it with both hands, agreeing to go for interview.

This was in the winter of 1956. It had been a particularly bitter one, and although I had enjoyed my work I was very dispirited about my prospects at the time. The other residents were more mature than I, and as well as enjoying their company I had the benefit of their encouraging attitude towards me. The companionship they offered me was tremendous so that when I told them I had been asked for interview at the Children's Hospital they were delighted. We went out to have a drink together. They gave me advice about interview technique, and drank my health perhaps too often, and assured me that I would be successful.

On the day of the interview there was a snowstorm. I had to take the early train to London, and for the journey I wore all my old clothes and sported a pair of borrowed gum boots. There was six inches of snow outside the hospital gates, and so I put my treasured best suit, my shoes, shirt and toilet bag into an old case and one of my friends took me to the station in his car. Carrying this rather battered portmanteau which was held together by a large piece of string, I took an early train to London. When I arrived there I went straight to the station hotel, and finding the gentlemen's toilet, washed, shaved, combed my hair, and changed into my new suit, taking the bus to my destination, a small Children's Hospital in the depths of a poorer part of London.

I arrived half an hour too early, self-consciously carrying my case, and after enquiring at the porter's lodge was shown into the waiting room. This was a dull and grimy place. The doors were painted brown, and the wallpaper, which at one time had been cream, was now peeling off in places. In the corners there was an occasional cobweb. There was a large table in the centre of the room, and chairs scattered around the walls. It was obviously the Board Room where the medical committee met at times. I took a seat at the end of the room facing the door and then went to the toilet, and shined my shoes again, and checked that my appearance was satisfactory, leaving my battered case behind. After a little while back in the waiting room two young ladies joined me, they were demure and well-dressed and quite good looking.

We introduced ourselves and one told me she had been a resident at a well-known teaching hospital in the North of England, having worked for a very famous paediatrician there. The other had been the resident at a famous teaching hospital in London. Although I knew my references were excellent I did not fancy my chances of getting this job very much after hearing all this.

Our waiting was interrupted by the entrance of a small figure, a lady of commanding presence. She wore a well-tailored suit and a shirt and tie. Her hair was tightly combed into a bun at the back. It was a mixture of brown and grey; she stood erect, and looked around the room. I realised that she must be someone of importance, and deferentially stood up by my chair, not quite knowing what to do about the suitcase. Our visitor glanced around the rather seedy board room and walked over to the first young lady, who was sitting near the door. She asked her about herself in a very gentle, quiet voice and in a rather caring manner. My first rival explained where she was from, and for whom she had been working. The elderly consultant was gracious and pleasant. She smiled and nodded, and wished her luck. She then approached the second candidate and did virtually the same thing. I stood there witnessing this, possibly with my mouth agape, and blushing, because I suddenly realised that this consultant was none other than one of my heroines, one of the foremost paediatricians in Great Britain. One of my teachers at medical school had told me all about her original work with deprived children in London, and I felt pleased to be in the presence of such an important person, who had not only contributed to medical science, but had also added a human sociological touch to paediatrics.

Naturally, I expected her to come over to me to repeat the process. She walked around the room, briefly looked out the window, approached me and, as I was wondering what to say, passed me by giving me a piercing look, as she did so, her face contorting slightly. She then turned on her heel and hurried out of the room. I felt horrified. Things did not look good again. Lady consultants obviously did not like me or so it seemed at the time. I would probably have to do locums for a spell, and see how things turned out. It had been an interesting trip up to London, anyway.

My thoughts were interrupted by the head porter who summoned in the first candidate. I being the last on the list. On her return, she looked rather flushed and a little flustered. I was too preoccupied by my thoughts to speak to her, and it occurred to me that it might be improper to ask her full details of the interview. When the second young lady returned from her interview, I noticed that she was almost crying. I wondered what awaited me. When I was called and ushered in, I found that the chairman was a clerical gentleman, the local vicar. He was pleasant, and things seemed to be going reasonably well. One of the interviewers, the head of the laboratory, asked me about my degree in biochemistry, and the other, obviously a paediatrician who wore a monocle, asked me a great deal about my work at the peripheral hospital. I did not know that he had been very friendly with one of the medical secretaries there, who I gather had telephoned him when she had heard that I was applying for a job. I shall always be grateful to that lady who I had befriended when her sister had been admitted to hospital with cancer. This was a bit of luck that I did not know about at the time.

When I returned to await the result of the interview I found two rather disconsolate young ladies sitting there. The first who had come from a teaching hospital in the North of England said that one interviewer was not at all happy when she told him for whom she was working. They were enemies of old, and he had openly said that he disagreed with the man's theories. I thought that this was a bit unfair, and rather off-putting, but at the time I needed a job. The second young lady had been asked where she had done her student obstetrics and she gave the same consultant's name. He then asked her whether she attended all the rounds on the new-born babies that they had delivered, and she affirmed that she had. He turned to her, said that he had never seen her there, in fact he was the paediatrician in charge of that unit and remembered that she had never come to ward rounds despite all efforts to find her when she was a student. Things were looking more hopeful for me, and indeed within a few minutes I was called back and offered the job.

I had imagined my duties would be in the main children's hospital, but almost casually I was told that, in fact, it was a small branch of a hospital in the Docklands area, servicing a very deprived population. This was something of a let down and a disappointment to me. However, I was no longer unemployed and when I had done my job in paediatrics, I would get a job in obstetrics, go into general practice and be my own master. I went back to join my friends at the district hospital. We went out to have a drink together and they cheered me up by saying that a training in paediatrics would be very useful for me in general practice and they were sure I would make a very good family doctor.

The small hospital to which I was sent is now (of course) closed. It was a happy one, where there were two resident junior doctors, a resident medical officer and a senior resident. They are still friends of mine today. Although it was a pleasant place and did good work, the staff of the main branch looked down on it and upon those who worked there, but I did not care because I was learning a lot, and I enjoyed working with the children and their parents. I was somewhat disconcerted however to find that several of my predecessors had left early and without references because the two chiefs there were thought to be somewhat difficult. Indeed, my chief, the man with the monocle, was a rather outspoken man, but of some clinical brilliance. His demands were high and one had to know every detail of the patient off by heart, at ward rounds, reciting these to the medical students, both undergraduate and postgraduate.

The other chief was universally feared. The preparations for his ward rounds were done with anxiety and tension. I have never forgotten the first one that I attended when I was two minutes late. My shoes clattered over the wooden floor of the ward when I approached the assembled throng surrounding the cot of an unfortunate child. He turned on me and asked me who I was. He had not been at the interviewing committee. When I told him that I worked with the other chief he told me to leave immediately because I had been late. Actually, I felt that I had been let off lightly. I was always early for his ward round after that, but was studiously ignored. He had the nasty habit of asking the most difficult questions, and would either snarl or make sarcastic remarks if the correct answers were not forthcoming. He was tall and handsome, but his style ruined his appearance and he seemed to have no friends. The only person who he seemed to get on with was the old pharmacist in the hospital, who had known him when he had been a resident there many years previously.

Every few months he would undertake a grand round. About twenty post-graduate students from abroad would attend. It would take up most of a Wednesday morning. The previous weekend and Monday and Tuesday were hives of activity, when my colleague would get the patients ready and prepare for this event. There was universal apprehension around the hospital beforehand, because these ward rounds could be quite traumatic to the staff. However, the chief was quite pleasant to the visitors who might come from all over the world. Anyway, he had not bothered me up until then and I felt fairly safe.

Therefore bright and breezy, I joined the assembled throng. When we got to the third patient I found myself near the front leaning on the side of the patient's cot. This child had a disorder of the white cells of the blood. I knew something about this, having read about it in the journal by chance some weeks before. I was busy with my thoughts, and miles away, when I suddenly found everybody looking at me.

"I am giving Pentose Nucleotide to this patient." I woke from my reverie with a start and reflexively answered,

"Of no value whatsoever, Sir."

The senior resident and the resident medical officer were on the other side of the cot to me. Their faces suddenly looked tense, and they went pale. The experienced ward sister frowned. Had I done the tactless thing again?

"Why do you say that?" I sighed audibly and said that although it had been undertaken twenty years before, recent research papers indicated that it had no effect on the disorder from which the child was suffering. I was however able to quote the exact reference.

This handsome man had a magnificent set of teeth and he showed them now in a snarling grin. He shrugged his shoulders, looked around, sniffed, bent down slightly and then stood erect before moving off to the next case without saying a word. He ignored me afterwards.

It was his habit after these ward rounds to go down to the pharmacy to see his only friend. We would always wait outside the door of the pharmacy dutifully, sometimes up to ten minutes, standing around and wondering what he was doing. On this occasion he collected his bag from his own house physician, gave me a piercing look and went straight out to the hospital car park and drove off.

The senior resident and resident medical officer mentioned casually that they would like to speak to me, and have an informal chat after lunch. It was not unpleasant. Again, I was given a short lecture on being tactful and not being too outspoken. 'Foot-in-mouth disease' was mentioned. I was told about other residents who had left the hospital without references and was reminded that if I made this particular chief unhappy it would reflect upon the happiness of the other members of the hospital. It was all very pleasant and gentle, and I felt quite uneasy afterwards

During that afternoon it was my duty to serve the Casualty Department at the Hospital and I buried my thoughts and disappointment in the work which I enjoyed. Tea was not provided by the nursing staff and was taken in the Pharmacy. At 4 o'clock I went there for a short break and must have looked rather fed up. The Pharmacist, an elderly man who always had a smile and was balding and pleasant, asked me to sit down. He was first class at his job and gave me some excellent advice. He always recounted stories about some of the consultants, describing their clinical and non-clinical habits and attachments, and I was always amused. He had a calming influence on people and we had a common interest in tea. I could always recognise the brand he was using, and cricket was often our subject for conversation in the few minutes we had together.

It was not to be like that today. Mr Maxwell the pharmacist was in a very good mood.

"Of course you made a very big hit this morning. The chief came down here, and told me that one of the juniors had informed him that the drugs he prescribed were useless. I asked him which one it was, and he mentioned Pentose Nucleotide. I told him there was none available. He asked me why, and I said that it was not in stock at the wholesalers. He asked me why again and I told him it was not being manufactured any more. He asked me why again, and I told him it have been proven to have been of no use. This was an eye opener to him, and I think you will find you made a hit with him because you seemed to know more than he did, and he likes that sort of thing." This was perfectly true and after that I could do no wrong. This man, who had been so unkind to me previously, now consulted me about a large number of things, including current research. He kept me on my toes and I was always wondering what he would ask me next, but it became a very good intellectual exercise for me, and I kept a close eye on his patients, looking at points of interest and detail and the current literature. The senior resident and the resident medical officer did not know what to make of this, and they left me alone. They were nevertheless very pleasant, but they had not experienced this sort of thing before.

The other chief, to whom I had a greater allegiance, was not so knowledgeable but was meticulous in his care of the patients. He had a good pair of hands, good eyes and good hearing. I remember we had a child with a very severe heart disease who had been in hospital for three months. All the valves of her heart were affected. I got to know the parents and gathered from them that they lived in very deprived circumstances. The mother told me that the girl had been sleeping on the floor in a box-room with her uncle on the bed. He had been lodging with the family, and contributed to the household expenses. The father was unemployed, but the uncle had a job as a labourer and his income was very important for the family finances. They were grossly overcrowded. They invited me around to their little flat, and I saw the damp walls, the poor furniture, and the lack of bathroom and toilet facilities. The lavatory was in a landing outside the flat, and in the winter it was extremely cold and damp. As one entered the block of flats one could smell the odour of unwashed bodies. It was very depressing and I wondered whether I would go into general practice in such an area. It might be a good thing, but it would be a battle to help such people. It would need a social crusade.

On every ward-round the consultant was worried about the damage the rheumatic fever had done to the red-headed child's heart. He suggested she go to convalesce for a few weeks and come back for reassessment. When she returned the social worker on the ward round said she was unhappy that the child should be returned to her terrible home conditions. At that time there was a long housing list, and people who lived in slums could wait many years for suitable alternative accommodation even when helped by medical certificates. The family was on two housing lists, the local council and the city authority.

I spoke to the parents about this again after the ward round, and they told me they felt they had little chance of being re-housed. This was because it had been discovered that they were boarding out the mother's brother illegally, and were over-crowded because this man was staying in their little flat. They knew the council as corrupt, but they had not got even enough money to bribe the appropriate council officials. I was prepared to discount what they said at the time and did not want to get involved in those deep and treacherous waters.

On the next ward round I explained the problems to the chief in general. He was quite upset about what was going on, and as far as he was concerned, the child would not go home until the family was properly re-housed. After the ward round, I was sitting in the residents' common room recovering and had what I felt was a bright idea. I consulted Janet our Scots ward sister, who was a woman of infinite wisdom and clinical experience. She agreed that my idea might be worthwhile. I did not consult my senior colleagues but got on the phone to the offices of the city authority and asked to speak to the chief medical officer. I was put through to his secretary immediately. She told me he was not available. I went around to Janet, our ward sister, invited her back to the residents' sitting room, and managed to persuade her to telephone the secretary again and say that she was the chief medical officer's wife and that she wished to speak to him urgently. She was put through immediately. He came on the telephone and with trembling hands she passed the receiver over to me. I immediately explained to this medical knight that I had used deception to gain contact with him, and felt I should speak to him urgently. He listened. I told him the story of this very unfortunate child in detail. I added that my chief would not allow the child out of hospital until the family was re-housed. I was surprised that he was so receptive and understanding. He made a note of the name and address and wrote down a few details as I dictated to him, and asked me to tell my chief that the child would be re-housed within three weeks. He wanted to be assured that this message would be passed on.

One week later, on the ward round, when we got to the bed of this unfortunate child I was able to tell the chief and the other members of staff with some degree of triumph, that the family was going to be re-housed within three weeks. The chief looked a little surprised and asked me what had happened. I explained to him that I had telephoned the chief medical officer of the city authority. Sister Janet was blushing at the time. I also said that he had sent a personal message to the chief saying that I was to reassure him that the family would be re-housed in three weeks. The chief asked me again how this had happened, and I said I had merely telephoned. He was about to wash his hands, and beckoned me to the end of the ward to the sink there. He said nothing, and after he had dried his hands, he re-inserted his monocle.

"Did you know the chief medical officer is my brother in law? Did you know that he is not married, and did you know that he was extremely amused and impressed by you? I think you did very well but would you mind not doing it again without letting me know."

I actually blushed and was very happy. At this time, my senior resident and the resident medical officer had no idea what to make of me. Janet winked and I decided once and for all to be a paediatrician.

Gawley

Lionel told me this story. I am sure it's true. If it isn't it should be. The Jews in this small town in the valleys of South Wales had been established some twenty to twenty five years. They had become quite prosperous as shopkeepers, tally men, small artisans and had moulded themselves into a small community with a synagogue and cantor.

They even had their own tramp. He was a strange fellow, named Gawley. Half German by descent, it was said that he had been to university but was frustrated, rejected in a love affair and had decided to go on the road. We don't see many tramps these days and Gawley was relatively high class because he spoke so well with a half Welsh accent and he had the gift of the gab. Despite this he was not popular. He would arrive at the homes of the wealthier on Friday evening, just as they were sitting down for their Sabbath meal and would try to join in. One time they tried to pay him off but this did not seem to work since he took up drinking and became an embarrassment to everyone. The only people who seemed to have any pity on him were the Rabbi and the Cantor and one or two others who were relatively poor and would give him bread and cheese sandwiches. It is thought that he had some money because every now and again he would deck himself out in second-hand clothes although these were probably given to him by various people to get rid of him.

Apart from him the only other problem that the community had was the fact that if a member had died, the nearest suitable graveyard was some twenty five miles away and it took a whole day to inter the beloved one who then seemed so far away.

They clubbed together and bought a plot of land just outside the town and there was a ceremony of dedication attended by dignitaries and notables. The ground was consecrated at an impressive ceremony and everybody left happily.

I think it was a good thing that no one seemed to die for years after this and longevity reigned supreme.

The first person who was eventually interred there was Gawley. He was knocked over by a lorry at night. Of course there was no one to pay for the funeral and the rabbi and cantor were the only people who attended. Although everybody was not so unkind about Gawley they seemed to have pressing reasons not to go to this particular funeral. Most of them had other engagements along the valley, were unwell or were too busy. Only one person admitted that he wouldn't go to the funeral of that old chap because he was a drunkard. Gawley was duly buried in the new cemetery. It was sad that only two people attended apart from him.

Time and tide took their toll on this little town. Some of the Jews became successful and moved out; some moved off to larger towns and after another thirty years none was left. The town prospered, however, and was still pleasantly situated in the valley. The lilting Welsh tones of the inhabitants could be heard in the chapel and life went on as before but the Jews were no longer there.

You know how it is. It is popular now to go back to one's roots and the rabbi's son summoned his brother. Both were successful. They had moved up to London, but thought it might be an idea to visit the old place. A broad motorway took them there in a matter of four hours, and along the main street they quickly located the now derelict, closed and barred synagogue. There was however, a caretaker around. He was young, fair haired, and rosy cheeked, pleasant and somewhat strangely he still wore a peaked cap. But then he was a caretaker of other institutions as well. He was found. He was helpful. He was informative. He opened up the building and they looked, smelled and poked around and pushed away cobwebs. They sat down in the seats that they had sat in for the Sabbath morning service, stood on the pulpit where their father had given his fiery sermons and reflecting on past things smiled at each other. They had a tear for those wonderful happy days and sad days gone by, and thought about all the people they had known worrying where they had gone and what had happened to them. They went into the class rooms where they had been taught. They sat in the creaky desks – it was a tight fit now – and thought about how life had changed. They discussed their father's struggles for the community and all of their misdemeanours of childhood, and were about to go when the caretaker reminded them that there was another place of Jewish interest in the town. This was the cemetery.

"I thought you should come to the cemetery because there is something very interesting there that you should know about," he explained in his Welsh lilt.

"I wonder if you gentlemen would help me in this." He seemed to be searching. He would say no more and was determined to take them to the cemetery. They were a little puzzled and drove him up there. He opened the gate. The whole area was covered by grass which had been cut and looked after. It was in the form of a small hill and in the middle of the hill looking down was only one grave with a headstone. It was the only grave in the cemetery. No one else had been buried there. They walked up to the grave and on it carved in stone was the name of Gawley. Otherwise it was completely bare. There was no further information but the grave had been tended. It was obvious that none of the inhabitants of the town wanted to be buried in the same cemetery as Gawley. Was this class prejudice or mere snobbery? The two brothers were both thinking about this and the caretaker spoke again.

"He must have been a very important man to be buried here on his own and to have the whole cemetery to himself. Who was he?"

Well he might well ask!

Feltsham

I had been in practice in Feltsham for about ten years. I felt that I had been lucky to be the village doctor in the place where I had been brought up myself. I knew most people and they seemed to like me. It was not a very busy practice but an interesting one and it was a delightful part of the world in which to live. Our village was one where people lived for a long time. Anybody who had resided there for less than five years was regarded as an outsider, or a foreigner. People were rather nosey and found out as much as possible about newcomers and rather kept a distance from them for some time. There was a certain amount of snobbery about and though I kept clear, I was aware of it.

There was a manor house just up the road from the village but the owner was not the squire. He did, however, let out a lot of property in the district. Although we did not know young George well, we knew that his old father had had humble origins. Old George had built up his property business very gradually. He had started life in a small hamlet, Shelcombe, which is almost a mile and a half from the village. Old George had originally lived in one of the Elm cottages of which there were five, and he had been the owner of all of them but it was not for many years that the tenants realised who their landlord was. He used to employ a man from the local town to collect the rents. However, he would collect his rents himself, from our village and many people thought that he was a rent collector.

If there was damage to a property or if the roof leaked or the damp course was at fault they would complain to old George who invariably arrived with an old hat and an old gabardine raincoat and scuffed shoes. If they complained to George he would put on a wry smile and say,

"Well, I'll speak to the landlord, but you know that he is a hard man and it is more than my job is worth to complain too much." Old George was of course the landlord and he managed to conceal this fact for many years. It was not until he bought the manor house and had his son back from the public school that this was realised.

He was really quite a hard man and all the insults and snide remarks made to him in the local pub were like water off a duck's back. His son, young George, did try and improve the properties and we understood that he was doing quite well in the local town. The manor house was now quite well decorated and had space for three cars. There is a swimming pool and two tennis courts. Young George had three pleasant children, all of whom went to boarding schools, and a very pretty and charming wife.

Old George would live in the attic upstairs and had very little to do with the business these days. We thought that young George felt rather ashamed of him. Young George knew how to charge however and he was pretty rough on people who could not pay their rent. He was quite keen on evictions. He was however, generous in other ways and Chairman of the Governors of a small local preparatory school. He donated generously to it, supporting several scholarships. It was very difficult therefore to criticise him, although he was not really looked upon with great friendship by most people in the village.

I liked to make my own house calls and most often one could go on foot to see various patients. I dispensed my own drugs and was pretty aware of the qualities and disadvantages of the local consultants and even of the nursing staff and midwives.

We had a newcomer to the village in 1973. He was a young Irishman who was a school teacher and had gained employment at the preparatory school. I had no more than a nodding acquaintance with him. He tended to keep himself to himself. He brought his young son aged three to see me one day. The boy was seriously ill and I called an ambulance and referred them to the local City Hospital Paediatric Department. I did not hear from him for a week when he telephoned me from a public phone booth in Shelcombe Hamlet. He was distressed. He had discharged his son from the hospital after there had been an altercation with the Ward Sister. There had been some political discussion about Irish Nationalism. He had felt that his child was not getting the proper treatment and in a fit of pique he had taken the boy home. He said that his son had a high temperature and was perspiring and that the rash had reappeared and that he had not got any medicine and would I call. It was a spring afternoon and I took my bag and walked down to Shelcombe. It was a pretty little place and there were just a few houses scattered around the main road. The Irishman lived in one of the Elm Cottages and admitted me readily. He was somewhat agitated. He explained the situation to me and actually told me what was wrong with the child and what treatment he had been on. There was no telephone in the cottage and I had foolishly neglected to contact the City Hospital to find out what had happened before I made the home visit.

I asked to examine the child and was admitted to the bedroom. This was in an attic under the eaves of the roof. It was a sorry place for a child to be in. The roof was leaking, the ceiling showed damp patches and water had obviously been running down the inside wall. The paintwork was peeling; the windows were cracked and admitted a draught because the latches did not fit the frame properly. The young Irishman seemed unaware of this. I thought that we could manage the case at home with a daily visit and explained this to him but thought that the child should be moved downstairs to another room which was more healthy. He agreed to this and I commenced treatment. He asked me to telephone him but I said I would pop in the following day and look after the child myself after I had telephoned the hospital.

I wandered off home and telephoned the hospital the next day and it appeared that all I had to do was to continue treatment. I did not get involved with the political situation. I knew that the Ward Sister on the paediatric ward could be rather fierce with parents and there had been complaints from them before. So I was satisfied just to deal with the matter myself and thought that the child would be alright at home.

When I went the next day the child seemed to have settled down but I put it to the father that he ought to do something about the house. He told me that there was very little that he could do because he was on a poor income and was reluctant to complain about the landlord. Of course, the landlord was young George and he was Chairman of the Board of Governors of the school and the young Irish teacher was embarrassed and in difficulties over taking the owners to the Rent Tribunal or complaining. I understood the situation all too well. I thought possibly the Irishman could seek re-housing elsewhere and he promised to do so. We kept the child downstairs, and over the next few days he seemed to improve sufficiently for me to make visits every other day. The parents were most grateful.

I was coming home from one of the visits when my wife greeted me by saying that I had been called to the Manor House to see young George. He had been taken ill and he couldn't find his consultant who would come down periodically from the local town. He asked whether I would go and see him.

I had never been to the Manor House before and was reluctant to drive my rather shabby Mini Minor into the magnificent driveway where there were one Rolls Royce, one Jaguar and one Daimler parked already. That was apart from the Land Rover! The door was opened by the housekeeper who ushered me first into the library where I spoke to young George's wife. She was a charming lady, pleasant and helpful and gave the symptoms and apologised profusely for dragging me out. She explained the situation again and asked me to come up and see young George. He seemed pleasant although his manner was slightly diffident and a little superior. He was a small man with horn-rimmed glasses which he wore in bed. He had a small military moustache and bright red cheeks. His overall appearance was refined and exact. The bedroom was ornate. George was sitting up in a four poster and everything was just so, including the carpets and the curtains. Young George had got pneumonia and I explained this to him. He asked whether a chest x-ray was necessary and I said that I thought that I was satisfied with the diagnosis and that he would do well with antibiotics. I said that I would try and speak to his consultant the next day and tell him this and we could arrange for a consultant radiologist to come down and bring a portable x-ray machine if he insisted, but I was still quite satisfied with my diagnosis. Young George was not satisfied with this and he wanted the x-ray done. I therefore got on to a friend and arranged for him to come down forthwith.

I went home and came back because young George had demanded my attendance. The consultant radiologist confirmed my diagnosis and we showed the x-ray to young George. He asked me a lot of questions about pneumonia what the causes were, and whether he had got it from his wife. I think I was able to satisfy his questioning and explained all the side effects of antibiotics, but said that I did not think that he would have any, and that I would visit the next day because I was unable to contact his consultant physician. He agreed. I saw him daily for several days and after about four or five days he was up and about. He took me into his office and with a flourish to ask me what my fees were. I had always been diffident about charging fees to private patients and to my horror discovered that young George was on my National Health Service list, so I was unable to charge a fee. I explained this to young George who said that he did not know how to thank me and could he have another x-ray in a few days to make sure that things had cleared up. I had to agree to this and did so.

We had the x-ray and went through the ritual of showing it to young George. I was rather surprised when his wife asked me down to have tea with them. I was reluctant to accept the invitation because quite frankly I did not like young George, but I was also hungry, so I agreed. We sat down and the housekeeper served us. It was quite a pleasant tea, with scones, sandwiches and cake, and young George asked me about myself in a slightly patronising manner. He asked me what the people in the village were like and how they treated me because he always thought that they were rather standoffish with him. I told him I had had an interesting case recently of a child with a rare disease who had been sent home from the local hospital. Young George's wife frowned.

"Why was he sent home?" I explained the situation but did not say who the patient was. I told them that I had been able to visit every day and fortunately the child was better, but they lived in the most dreadful accommodation and it seemed quite wrong to me that a child of three should have his bedroom in an attic room with a leaking roof and water going down the walls and windows that let in the draught. Young George's wife was horrified by this. She said how upsetting it must be for the poor parents. I agreed with her. She explained that George's family had been in the property business for many years. I told her that I knew something about this, and said that my late father knew young George's father. They smiled at this. They seemed very proud. They explained what a wonderful landlord George was, how exact and careful he was and how he kept his books carefully and used his home for an office, apart from having an office in the local town. I explained that I had always enjoyed working in the village but occasionally had to go down to Shelcombe. I enjoyed the walk down to Shelcombe, but was distressed to find such dreadful living conditions in Elm Cottages, but of course I did not think this was one of young George's properties. Young George's face hardened.

"But it is one of mine!" It had slipped out without his realising it. I feigned embarrassment.

"Oh, I am so sorry, I didn't realise it was one of your properties, but can you do something about it?" Young George smiled and said,

"Well since you are not going to ask any fees I will have to go ahead and re-house the family." I thanked him. The family was re-housed and both young George and the Irish teacher's son got better.

About six months later there was a parcel outside my surgery door. It contained twelve Green Shield stamp books, all filled out. There was a note from the young Irish teacher. He had got another position. He wanted to show his gratitude and left me his savings. He never let me know where he was going so I could not write and thank him. He must have dropped the parcel in just as he was leaving the village. I exchanged the books of stamps for some silver plated candlesticks and when I look at them I remember the Irishman. Some of the silver has come off, but we still keep them on the sideboard. They help us remember.

The Smallest Condom

Mrs Kelly was anxious and tense on the telephone. Her brother-in-law Fred was in trouble. He needed her help. She had told him not to marry that divorcee, and as usual he had not listened to her. Could George help?

Trying to unscramble the following confused account on the phone was difficult but essentially it seemed that Fred's step-daughter had accused him of sexually interfering with her several times. The Police had been called in by Social Services and the case was to come up at the local Crown Court. Meanwhile Fred had lost his job. He was thoroughly depressed and would not discuss the matter with his sister-in-law or anyone else in the family. Could George help please? The defending solicitor would be pleased to contact him were he to agree.

Mary Kelly had been a good, thoroughly honest home help and had been with George's family for seventeen years. He could not refuse, but when the bundle of papers arrived it appeared that the prospects of success were poor in what appeared to be a difficult case.

The step-daughter was apparently an attractive girl of twelve. She was supported by her mother a rather outspoken blowsy blonde, George was told. Interference had taken place at least six times. The girl herself gave way to sobbing during giving evidence when she clearly gave her version of what had happened. Fred by contrast was reluctant to cooperate, nevertheless vehemently denying that anything of the sort had taken place.

Two doctors, one a police doctor, and the other a community paediatrician had seen the girl and had examined her. Although she complained that she had been penetrated, there was no local evidence of bruising bleeding or an infection in or around the external genitalia. Nevertheless, in their reports they supported her claim, citing evidence from a report from one of the Royal Colleges. George was dismayed by this.

He asked for a school report. This was helpful. Apparently the girl was aggressive and had been involved in fights with other school children including boys on several occasions. Her attendance record was also poor. Further enquiries were unrevealing.

He decided to speak to counsel who was a dignified middle aged lady. She was non-committal about prospects, but suggested that they ask for sight of the examining doctor's notes. This was to be allowed but only just before the case came up in court.

This was a bad time for George. His wife was ill, the car had broken down, and bills were accumulating. He was not prepared to pay for a taxi and decided to go to court by public transport. He was tired having spent the night before looking up the literature on previous cases. Essentially this case depended on whether he could prove that the so-called victim had not been penetrated. There was only the child's word for it. There was nothing in the research columns that was helpful. He made his way to the station but on a stroke of intuition popped into his local chemist shop on the way there.

The opposing doctor's notes were made available at the court and were revealing. Indeed, there was no evidence of trauma, but they had examined the child several weeks after the interference had been said to have taken place. The hymen was thick and the aperture half a centimetre in diameter. George went into court feeling more confident.

The opposing counsel was a blonde who flashed her teeth a great deal. She questioned the medical expert witnesses for the prosecution mainly on their opinion and experience. However, neither could explain the so-called victim's thick hymen when asked about it by counsel for the defence.

It was apparent that the judge was not impressed by these two gentlemen, and as they left the witness box he made a slightly sarcastic critical remark to each. George's turn was next. As he approached the witness box now with some apprehension, he fingered his inside pocket.

The opposing counsel's questions were easily dealt with. She smiled and so did George.

Defending counsel was actually not quite so easy at first. The question about the thick hymen was easily dealt with however. George explained to the court that it was caused by female hormones called oestrogens. One or two members of the jury actually nodded in agreement. Defending counsel then abandoned detailed questioning and requested George to make a statement to the court on why the child was not penetrated. This was the moment that he was waiting for. After reminding the court that the hymen was not ruptured and that the aperture in it was only one centimetre in diameter, he produced from his pocket a small packet containing a condom.

"There are no figures available from the medical literature of the size of the erect male penis. We do have the measurement of the hole in the girl's hymen however; it was half a centimetre. We do not have any measurements of the accused's external genitalia but this condom is the smallest size available. It is 3.5 centimetres in diameter, which is seven times that of the available space in the young female's hymen. Thus the smallest male penis could not effectively enter her vagina. It is therefore impossible for penetration to have taken place."

The jury remained passive but the judge smiled and nodded. He stopped the case. Fred was found not guilty. Mary Kelly was grateful.

SMART

I heard about Smart from two people; from Henry and from Frank. They were both scientists and fairly reliable. What I have to say about him is therefore pretty close to the mark. Henry often came round on a Saturday afternoon, and we would talk about the week, and people we had met and it would usually be a fairly pleasant and interesting discussion. I was pretending to be a scientist perhaps in a modest way at that time, and was anxious to pick up titbits about successful men.

The name was known to me because it had been in the newspapers when he won a famous international prize for his research. He had been made a Fellow of the Royal Society, and apparently had done all his work with an Irishman called White, while in a small private Institution that gave advice to those engaged in Atomic Research. White had been made professor in a Northern university, some years before, and was now quite well known. The scientific fraternity did not quite know what to do with Smart, and eventually he was given a position with research facilities at a famous national research institute.

Henry had met him there. Henry was somewhat amused by Smart. Apparently after the first few months, people in the institute saw very little of Smart. He always arrived late in the morning, carrying a small bulging, but shabby briefcase the straps of which were undone. Hardly speaking to anybody and just with the occasional curt nod to those who greeted him, he would make straight for his laboratory. Once he was in there, he slammed the door, and one could hear the key in the lock, and nothing was seen of him until about 5 o'clock in the evening, when he would make his way home. He would always walk down to the local pub, and disappear there for half an hour, and then make a beeline for the tube. He did not mix with the other scientists at all, did not go to the research meetings, did not publish any papers, and issued no reports to the institute for the first two years he was there. He was an enigma. Of course, people would talk about him. It was rumoured that he spent most of the day reading detective stories, and doing the crosswords of the major daily papers. Apparently he was always at his desk fiddling with something, and occasionally he spoke to his research assistant. He seemed to prefer to let this man get on with something himself, without very much direction. The latter fellow was often complaining, but he seemed to be happy with his sinecure, and after a while said nothing, but arrived on time, left on time, and also had nothing to do with the rest of the institute. Any letters that were sent to Smart by the director or colleagues were never answered, and the telephone was left off the receiver all day. People began saying that White had done all the work, and that Smart had horned in on it, and really he did not deserve all the honours he got, and that this had happened before to other people, and it was a disgrace and a scandal, but what could one do? The man had received a five year research grant, and it would be difficult to dislodge him. He was now accepted as part of the furniture, but with regret and some displeasure. We forgot about him. He was not worth talking about. His was one of the stories that got buried in the mass of interesting conversations that we had had with Henry and other friends on our Saturday afternoons around the tea table.

However, it was evident that Henry had something to say when he came around on the Saturday before Easter. There had been something of a scandal and an interesting development. Henry was agog to tell us what Smart had been up to. He obviously secretly admired the man, and was fascinated by him. Apparently Ferguson, a quiet, solid respectable scientist had gone to Smart to ask his advice. This had not been easy because Smart never answered the door. Nevertheless, Ferguson was determined and lay in wait for Smart one morning, accosted him at the entrance to the institute, standing in his way, and rather jocularly asked whether he could get his advice about something. It was evident that Smart was rather bad tempered in the mornings, because almost with a snarl, Smart said,

"All right then, come to my room at about eleven o'clock." So Ferguson duly went along at the appointed time, and was grudgingly admitted after the door had been noisily unlocked. The room looked tidy, but there were lots of papers all over the desk, and the assistant was busily making coffee in a corner, but seemed to be doing very little else. The assistant had a rather dreamy look about him, with a slight smile on his face.

"Well, how can I help you, old chap?" Smart seemed in a better temper. Ferguson explained his problem in theoretical physics. This related to an entirely different concept of the release of energy from an atomic pile. He explained that he had been working on this for three years, and felt that he was missing something, and wondered whether Smart had any ideas or thoughts. Secretly of course Ferguson was sorry for Smart. He knew that people looked down on the man now, and he thought that perhaps he could stimulate him to do something, and perhaps write a scientific paper. Ferguson had a sort of paternalistic approach to people. He was quite pleasant, although occasionally heavy and Smart, he felt, was a suitable subject for his paternal instinct. As Smart listened to Ferguson he wrote a few things down with a pencil on the back of an old envelope. After Ferguson had explained everything, Smart thought for a moment, and looking Ferguson straight in the eye, with a smile on his face, said,

"I think I can help you. I have been studying this subject for the last few weeks; it involves Smart's Dynamic Recalcitrant Theory. I think if one works at that it will give the answer." Ferguson did not wish to admit his ignorance. His Fellowship of the Royal Society came earlier than Smart's, and he felt himself something of an authority. He just nodded his head, and replied,

"Of course, you are quite right, I will work on it." He left the room rapidly and disappeared. He had a suspicion nevertheless that Smart was laughing at him behind his back.

The scandal came, Henry told us, two weeks later, when Ferguson in high dudgeon banged at Smart's door, and demanded entrance. Smart had to let him in because the noise was deafening. Ferguson burst in, sat down, looked Smart right in the face, and shouted at him.

"Smart, you are a fool. You were lucky to do so well internationally, but everybody believes that your colleague White did all the work on your famous report. You came here with a big research grant and every facility, and you have done nothing but sit in your laboratory, read detective stories and do crossword puzzles. You are a bad example to the juniors, and you have played practical jokes like a schoolboy. You should be ashamed of yourself and really you are not fit to work here."

Smart was apparently taken aback. He looked surprised and rather shaken.

"What are you moaning about?" Ferguson was still in high dudgeon.

"You know what I am talking about. You asked me to look up your theory two weeks ago, and I have looked at every reference and enquired from numerous colleagues. No one has ever heard of it. It has never been published. I came to you asking for genuine scientific advice and you, and probably your assistant, told me about some fantastic theory that has never existed, tried to make a fool of me, and I think you nearly succeeded."

Smart pulled back a chair, sat down, stretched out his legs sideways and laughed. Ferguson's face went red. He did not know quite what to do, or what to make of the situation, but his thoughts were interrupted by Smart, who giggled briefly and said,

"No, no old boy, you ran out of the room before I could explain it all to you. You are quite right. I have not published yet, but I have been thinking about it for some time. In fact, looking back, it has been at the back of my mind for several years."

Ferguson was taken aback. Smart went on,

"I think I have worked it out now, old boy, and if you will sit with me for half an hour, I will explain it to you, and this will solve your problem. I am so pleased to be able to help you, because you came just when the time was ripe, and just when I was completing my thoughts about the subject."

Ferguson sat motionless for a moment. He was visibly shaken by all this.

"Come on old chap, bring up your chair, and I will explain it all to you. I know the sort of things that you have been working on, and let me show you things I have done."

They sat down together at the desk, and after a while Ferguson realised that something he had been working on for many years, Smart had been able to solve on four small pieces of paper. All the information seemed to be in Smart's head. Ferguson soon lost his anger, and his understanding was followed by deep admiration for a man, who obviously had a fantastic intelligence, and scientific ability.

Henry told us that the first paper was a world-shattering one, and had revolutionised certain aspects of atomic physics. Smart insisted that his name was first, because as he explained, although Ferguson had the problem, he had found the solution, and he never published papers in alphabetical order. That is exactly what he had done with White. Incidentally, Smart began speaking to people in the institute, and would always refer to White, and would ask people how White was getting on, since he had not heard from him for some time. No one else had.

The effect on the institute was double fold. Smart's critics were stilled. They were put off when they realised that they had a colleague with tremendous ability who would produce work every five or ten years that would be world shattering. The juniors looked upon him with admiration. They could not get anything out of him, but still felt proud to be in an institution that survived with such a man in it. The director was delighted, and kept writing Smart notes of encouragement. He felt it would be very useful to have this in the annual report, but no one knows whether Smart actually sent a summary of his conclusions, or details for the annual report, although it was only briefly referred to, when the report was published.

I next heard about Smart from Frank who was a scientist and spent many years in research, but eventually was advised to go into industry. This was not to his scientific benefit, but was financially advantageous. It took a long time for Frank to settle down in industry, because the work was rather mundane. Frank would come round and see us intermittently, and it was always a pleasure to be with him, since he was lively. He tended to be critical of his fellow men, and although he was a good friend he made occasional jocular remarks about his colleagues' failures or disadvantages. He was not actually cruel, and did not really have a warped sense of humour, but enjoyed difficult situations in others.

We were having a drink with him one evening, when he told us about his new mentor, a Dr Smart, who had come to work as a consultant for his firm. This was in the early 1960s, and apparently Dr Smart's income as a consultant was £20,000 a year. For this Smart would arrive late on a Friday afternoon, and ask Frank about any problems. Smart would then sit down with him at a desk, with a stub of pencil, produce the answers, and tell him what to do. It appeared that Smart had no practical knowledge of any equipment, but could work out in mathematical terms what to expect. Most of his answers were fairly close to the mark, and although his visits were infrequent, the value of his advice was inestimable. He would be in the laboratory perhaps an hour or two, and then go home.

The firm changed hands, and a new managing director was appointed. He was clean- shaven, fair-haired, blue-eyed, red-cheeked and an enthusiastic rather bouncy young man. He told the staff that he was the new broom who was going to sweep the place clean. He interviewed everybody individually, including Frank. He seemed satisfied with Frank's work, but questioned him closely about the costs of the laboratory, and asked him about Smart. Apparently, he had written to Smart, and asked him to come for interview, but Smart had not replied to his letters. Frank was cautious in discussing his senior, and suggested that perhaps the managing director might like to accost Smart, when he came late on Friday afternoon. The managing director did this on the following Friday, because Frank could hear an altercation outside the laboratory door. He peeked out, and found the two men deep in conversation. The managing director's face was even redder, and Smart was looking dead-pan and seriously into the ground. The managing director was obviously attacking Smart verbally, and Smart was not responding. The noise outside died down, and

Frank retreated from the door, and busied himself. Smart came in and went through the usual ritual of answering questions and dealing with problems.

"Would you like to come and have a beer with me, it is nearly closing time for the laboratory?" he said. Frank thought this was a great honour. Smart was an unusual man and some of his brilliance might rub off. They walked round to the local public house, and went into the bar. Smart ordered Frank a half pint of ale and for himself he ordered two pints, and proceeded to consume these rapidly.

He opened up. "You know that young man is an ignoramus. He was trying to tell me how to do my job, He is not a scientist; he is one of these efficiency experts. In the long run they don't do any good. They never really earn their own money. I expect he'll try and get me the sack or dismiss me."

Frank said nothing and continued to listen.

"Of course, it is not like working in the place where I was before. There were a few gentlemen there. I remember Ferguson. He was quite a distinguished scientist, and I could get on with him. The director was not too bad. I suppose in the end he was understanding, but really working for this young man who called himself the managing director is impossible; still I expect they will give me the sack."

They parted company since Smart did not ask Frank for another drink, and had consumed two pints already. A week later Smart came into the laboratory smiling happily to inform Frank that he had been dismissed.

"Would you like to come and have another beer with me?" Frank agreed, although he thought it might be dull. This time as they walked into the pub, Frank got in first.

"I think I'll have a gin and tonic, I fancy one." Smart shrugged his shoulders and ordered it, and his usual two pints. They sat down at the same table, and Smart opened up again.

"Do you know they came along to the house that went with this job and tried to evict my tenant? I had to get my solicitor onto them you know. They thought that I shouldn't have tenants, but obviously they hadn't read the small print in the agreement when they took me on. It was stated quite clearly there that I could come and go when I liked to the lab, and I was merely a consultant, and if they gave me the sack, the house was mine, and nothing in the agreement said that I couldn't have my tenants in it, you know. My wife and I live out in the country in a much nicer house than theirs. We had a small income from the tenants, but they were really young people I felt sorry for. He was a newly-qualified scientist, obviously very clever, and I thought that if we accommodated him nicely, it would help him in his work. He has just got his Ph.D.

They actually sent a man in to try and evict him. They didn't waste any time. I thought it was very rude of them, but of course they've learnt their lesson now, because under the terms of the agreement, when I signed up with your firm, if they gave me the sack, and dismissed me, the property reverted to me. I suppose it's a bit of luck. I did not resign, they dismissed me. Still, I am sure the firm can afford it."

We listened to Frank, and told him what we had heard about Smart before. We were not surprised that this man was not only a great intellect, but was worldly wise, and had always carefully paid great attention to detail. At the institute his nickname was 'Lucky Jim'. We thought he was rather smarter than that.

One Good Turn Deserves Another

When Elliot felt depressed he used to walk to Kingsway in Holborn and take a tram to Purley in Surrey. He would take the front seat of the upper deck, so that somehow the swaying rhythm of the vehicle would soothe his troubled and anxious mind. On that day it was raining, cloudy overhead and rather steamy inside the tram but the top deck was otherwise empty apart from an old man who sat alone right at the back. In the past Elliot had sometimes accosted people on the tram and got talking to them. Occasionally, conversations were interesting but now his mind was pre-occupied with failure in his examinations. He had just received the results of his last attempts.

He had managed to obtain a place at university and had done well in geology, but when it came to the final B.Sc. examination he had failed repeatedly the subsidiary subject of Botany. He knew that he would not get an honours degree and if he did not pass the botany practical which he had failed so often, he might not get anything at all. This was a let down because his younger brother had got an honours degree in physics, and although most of the family did not mind, it hurt Elliot's pride that he did not pass this wretched botany practical examination, and be freed from the hours of study. He would not be able to do research in geology which he enjoyed although most of his professors seemed to think that he had an original mind and he was at a loss what to do to further his career.

As the tramcar weaved its way through the cobbled streets of south London his mind was temporarily diverted by the scenes around him. He had brought a knapsack, had a few sandwiches and a flask of coffee and planned to trudge down and eventually get to the South Downs, walk around a bit and come home late in the evening no doubt refreshed.

The tram reached its destination and Elliot got up and walked to the back of the upper deck of the vehicle. He saw that the only other passenger was a rather elderly man with white hair. He was small and slightly bent and was wearing an old stained raincoat. Elliot made to let him go down the stairs first, but the old man insisted that Elliot precede him. Without further ado Elliot plunged down the stairs. The rain had stopped and he was ready for the road. He alighted from the tram and stood on the pavement taking a breather. The old man had had some difficulty in getting down the stairs and as he tried to get off the tram, for some unknown reason the vehicle jerked forward. The old man tumbled backwards and fell into the road. The conductor seemed to take no notice and the tram started off on its way. The old man was left in the road. He had banged his head and although he was not knocked out he was obviously in some pain. He seemed to be able to move his limbs. His mackintosh was soaked with water and knowing his first-aid, Elliot told him not to try to get up yet, and made sure that all the limbs were sound. He then picked the old man up and dusted him down. The old man had a high, querulous voice and said his name was Ormsby. There was no one else around, and Elliot asked whether he could be of further assistance.

"Well, you could help me get a taxicab; I still have some distance to go." Looking at him rather closely Elliot realised that the old man's face was pale but quite refined. The nose had a slight beak to it, was shiny and the cheekbones were high. The eyes were green but alert. Elliot picked up the old man's hat and dusted it down as well. The old man refused to wear it however. They looked along the road and there was a taxi rank 100 yards due south. He helped him there and again waited with him for a taxi to arrive at the rank. They had to wait for about ten minutes before one arrived. Elliot said that he would help the old man into the cab, but Ormsby seemed to think that he might also have some trouble when he got to his own residence, since there was no lift and there were some stairs to climb. He asked Elliot whether perhaps he would come home with him, and he would gladly give him a cup of tea. Elliot obliged. It was a short journey; the old man was quite silent. They got to quite a reasonable block of flats and he manoeuvred the old man through the gate and up two flights of stairs, obtained the key and opened the door. The flat was quite a pleasant one, with lots of books around and obviously antique furniture that was well polished. Ormsby lived on his own. He must have been some sort of academic at one time Elliot thought, and he certainly made a good cup of tea. It was beginning to rain again, but Elliot was determined to get to the Downs despite the weather, and giving the old man his telephone number and giving his general practitioner a call so that he could be looked over at some time, he bade farewell.

Ormsby was profuse in his thanks and said that he hoped that they would meet again. It struck Elliot at the time that the old man was rather a lonely person and since he was rather incommunicative he felt that he might need brighter company at some timc. He made a mental note of this, thinking that perhaps he would go and visit him again. However he never managed to do so. The rain was now pouring down and Elliot decided not to go any further. He managed to get a bus to the tram stop, and took another tram back to Kingsway. The whole day had been a disappointment to him. As he arrived back in London thoughts of the dreadful examination came back to him and thoughts of failure returned.

He walked through the streets of Bloomsbury and found a small cinema bought a ticket and saw *The Blue Angel* for the fifth time. This film suited his state of mind because it was about an academic who was very clever and falls for a blonde who virtually destroys him. Elliot felt in a revengeful mood about examiners most of the time.

He did not really put his mind to study or to practice, before attending the University examination hall several months later. This time the papers did not seem too bad but he looked forward to the practical examination with dread. Predictably it was pretty bad. He had to cut sections of plants and his hands trembled with the razor when he used it His staining looked awful under the microscope, he could not identify various unclassified specimens, and the experiments he set up did not seem to work. He knew that things were going badly.

In the middle of an examination sometimes there is a moment of stillness. This usually occurs when the head examiner comes in so that he is available to answer any queries from the candidates. This usually happened about an hour after the examination had started. It did not happen this time, but Elliot, who was sited near the main entrance in this very large laboratory and examination hall, did notice a flurry at the door and one of the technicians entered. Then three men came in, two tall ones and a short one. The short one was rather elderly and for a moment Elliot thought that he knew him. The procession walked round all the benches, nodded to all the candidates and asked if everything was all right. Elliot was the last. His mind was racing. He knew this man. The examiners came to his bench which was a mess. While he was looking through the microscope the elder and presumably the senior turned to him unexpectedly and quietly whispered to him, "One good turn deserves another." It was as if this message had come out of thin air. By the time Elliot dared turn round again the examiner had gone.

He did his best with the answers and the specimens that he had to present and left them on the bench. He felt a little peculiar as he walked out but went over to one of the laboratory assistants and asked who the senior examiner was; the rather short elderly man.

"Oh, that's Professor Ormsby, he's the Chief Examiner."

Elliot passed.

Izzy

Unfortunately, Izzy had underestimated the requirements for Medical School entrance. He was untutored in the art of making such an application. He was also naively honest so that in the section of the application form asking for interests outside purely academic subjects, he wrote that one of his sports was ping-pong and that he was no longer a member of the Communist Party. He made twelve applications, all delivered by hand and all accompanied by a silent prayer. All were rejected.

He went to seek the advice of his old comrade Alf Brown. They had a cup of tea together while they discussed the situation. Eventually between them they agreed on what to do next. At first Alf suggested that Izzy applied to one of the Medical Facilities outside London.

"The competition in the provinces is not so great. You would stand a better chance that way," he said. Izzy was not enamoured of the idea. There were difficulties. He lived with and was supported by his sister, and would not be able to afford lodgings. He had an evening job in London and was barely able to manage on the income from this.

"What about Glasgow?" suggested Alf. "I know of several chaps of your religious persuasion who have got places there. They are not so prejudiced in Scotland, you know." Izzy again demurred. He could not even afford the railway fare. Alf thought again.

"Of course, I didn't go straightaway into one of the major teaching hospitals myself, you know. I did my basic medical course at King's College London before doing my clinical training and working with patients at one of the teaching hospitals. Of course, why didn't I think of it beforehand? You should apply to King's or a similar institution and if you pass the examination in basic medical science you will stand a chance at one of those halls of medical learning. If my memory serves me correctly old MacKay is still the Dean of the medical faculty there. He always had a soft spot for the underprivileged and is a bit of a left winger. I was one of his prize pupils and he did once ask me to take up Physiology. But I told him that I would do better work at the bedside by healing the sick. I did send him a letter from Barcelona when I was in the International Brigade in Spain. I wonder if he remembers? I suppose I could send him a letter of introduction for you. I am not sure whether it would do any good, but there is nothing to lose. I'll do it! Get an application form and I'll help you fill it out."

Izzy was grateful and agreed. The application form was duly obtained, filled out and submitted, and as usual delivered personally, and as advised by Alf was accompanied by a hand-written covering letter.

This time Izzy was successful. He was admitted. He was not even asked for an interview. The course was more strenuous and demanding than he had initially envisaged but he worked hard. The hours of study were long. He also had to keep up appearances and buy text books. This meant that he would spend most of the weekends at his part-time job and had to study his medical subjects in the evenings. The text books were expensive so he searched for second-hand ones. He also used the library in the college for study. Fares, clothes and footwear needed to be budgeted for. He found that if he got up early he could save the fares to the college by walking there. He did this every morning and was always on time for the lectures and demonstrations. He approached the college via the Embankment from the east. He often caught sight of the Dean, Professor MacKay, who was apparently also an early riser. He was a brisk walker and approached from the west. If they met, Izzy never failed to offer a deferential morning greeting. This was always met with a nod of the head.

It took some time for Izzy to attune himself to the demands of student life. He was now twenty two years old. He could not engage in sporting and social activities which leaven the burdens of the undergraduate life. He could ill afford such luxuries. His suit was second-hand and he took off his footwear as soon as he got home to save on the shoe leather. He paid his college fees in cash at the end of each term. He was always meticulous about this.

There were occasional moments of unexpected embarrassment. One of his fellow students enquired which Public School he had attended, another suggested that he used a different tailor and shirt maker. He always managed to pass off these queries and comments.. There was one fellow student whom Izzy sensed was also not very well off. Jab was younger and a companionable and sensible chap. Sometimes Izzy and he would leave college and walk to the bus stop together. Izzy would see Jab off and trudge his weary way home by himself. Hc felt too ashamed to tell Jab that his own limited budget did not even allow him the luxury of a bus ride. Nevertheless, he felt that Jab was a sympathetic fellow and in their short associations he felt comfortable.

All went reasonably well. Most of all, he loved the work. He now realised that he had chosen the right course and the right profession. Increasingly, he managed to keep up with the course work. He did not shine, but he passed all of the college examinations.

A slight crisis arose before the last term. He had to pay for both the examination fees to the University and his tuition fees together, and he did not have quite enough cash to pay for both. Several bank managers did not view his prospects favourably, and not one of them was possessed of a sufficiently generous disposition to take a risk on Izzy's future career. After all, even if he passed the next exam, it would be three more years before he qualified as a doctor. It was too much of a risk and anyway Izzy had never really held down a proper job.

He took a chance, deposited some funds in a bank account, was able to write a cheque and sent this off with his application to the University Examination Board. He avoided the college bursar's office as far as he could, and decided to pay the college fees as soon as funds became available. He did this and passed the examination. Three weeks later he appeared at the bursar's office with his new cheque book, apologised for the oversight and wrote out a cheque for the previous term's fees. The clerk behind the desk seemed a little confused about this.

"Mr Bogdanofsky, the account register shows that your fees have already been met. Excuse me a moment, I shall have to speak to the Bursar about this. Please take a seat, this will take a moment."

Izzy was a bit bothered about this. Had he paid already? Perhaps his sister had secretly done so, but he had not told her about this slight difficulty. She had been too generous with her small income already. He kept his nerve and waited. He had not long to wait. The bursar soon arrived. He was gentlemanly and apologised for keeping Izzy waiting. At that moment Izzy reflected that attitudes at the college were far different from the insults and bad language he had put up with when he was looking for work some five years previously. It all seemed so long ago and far away now.

The Dean wanted to see him. Would he go upstairs to the Dean's office. He would see him now. Izzy was still puzzled but he went as bidden to do so. MacKay's office was small and dark. The Dean bade Izzy sit down.

"I am sorry that we have never had the opportunity to meet personally before, Mr Bogdanofsky," he said..., "but I am sure that you realise that with so many students in our courses and the cares of my office, there is not always the time. Of course, I have had occasion to meet some of your fellow students but these were in unfavourable circumstances when there were difficulties and problems." Izzy must have looked a little worried at this remark, but MacKay went on to reassure him.

"I did remember your name however. It does stand out rather. Brown wrote to me about you when you first applied for entrance here. I was impressed by his letter. I was quite fond of Brown, you know, and would have liked him to have joined my department, but he went on to better things and on reflection he was right. You know he wrote to me from Barcelona when he was in the middle of the Spanish Civil War. He's an idealist and they are few and far between these days. Most of my students have ideas of grandeur. They want to go into private practice. I don't think that you are that sort of chap. By the way, I used to see you on my way to college walking along the Embankment. It was good exercise. How long did it take you to get here every morning from Bethnal Green? It's about five miles, isn't it?"

Izzy was bemused. All was known! Nevertheless, he kept up appearances and responded by saying that he enjoyed the walk, and that it took about an hour and a half.

"By the way, I closed your college account myself. I have a small fund for this and anyway I knew that you would pay up. By the way, you'll have to find a place in one of the teaching hospitals to do your clinical work, to walk the wards and that sort of thing. You had better start applying soon or you will miss your chance. You can use me as a referee. I'll support you. Good day, and the best of luck!" Izzy thanked the Dean profusely and as he staggered out, he was almost in tears.

Izzy had always kept Alf in touch with his progress. He still occasionally popped in for a Friday evening meal. Although Alf's mother was a very good cook and now plied him with her delicacies, she still had her doubts about him. He put it to Alf during dinner that he still had problems. There were only three medical schools that took undergraduate students from King's at this stage of their studies. His friend, Jab, had got the last place at one of them, and his applications at the other two had been put in but he had heard nothing as yet. He had telephoned the school secretary at one and he had not been at all hopeful about his chances. The ugly thought of anti-Semitic prejudice had crossed his mind. Alf wisely suggested that they took a walk over to Hyde Park to discuss things on the following Sunday. Hyde Park was a favourite venue for the insolvent and underpaid in those days. Alf usually went there to heckle the Fascist speakers. He was quite good at this but occasionally there were scuffles and trouble. Izzy therefore suggested that they take a walk along the Serpentine, a lake at the other end of the park.

Alf was also troubled by the possibility that religious prejudice might impair Izzy's chances. He had researched all the medical schools in London and had found that the Dean of one of the two in which Izzy's applications were still being considered had a Jewish sounding name.

"Why don't you take the bull by the horns and go and see that Dean? Ask for a personal interview yourself. He can only say no, and it might even help."

Izzy had another idea. He wrote to his old Dean, Professor MacKay, and asked him to write a letter to this gentleman suggesting that he see Izzy personally. MacKay agreed and when Izzy telephoned the medical school a week later an appointment was arranged. Meanwhile Alf had fitted Izzy out with a new suit and a new pair of shoes. He decided to accompany him on the journey there to give him confidence.

The Dean was a small person, his office was even smaller than that of MacKay. He looked hard at Izzy and in rather peremptory tones asked him why he had come. His attitude was unexpected. He seemed busily preoccupied and at first somewhat uninterested. Izzy did not quite know how to put it to him that he was worried that his application might not be favourably considered. After all, who was he to ask! What indeed had he to offer? Nevertheless possibly because he was a little angry at this reception, he let go at full blast. The Dean stopped him in mid sentence. Izzy noted that apart from having cultured tones, he had a marked lisp.

"Where did you learn to speak like that?" he asked. Izzy had been in full flow so that his rejoinder of, "Like what?" came quite naturally.

"With an Oxford accent," was the reply. "I went to elocution classes when I was eighteen years old," Izzy said.

"Oh, I didn't expect you to have such a refined accent when MacKay rang me up about you." Izzy thought for a moment. So MacKay hadn't written. Was this better or worse? His thoughts were interrupted by another peremptory question.

"If you are as poor as he claims that you are, how is it that you are wearing such a good suit?" This was easy.

"My best friend bought it for me so that I would be presentable at this interview." The interrogation went on.

"How do you know him? Who is he? What does he do for a living?" Izzy decided to tell the Dean the whole story, all about his leaving school as being uneducable, all about his unemployment, his failure as a cabinet maker and that his life had changed once he could see properly. He did not mention the Communist Party. He felt he could safely leave that out. The Dean's attitude softened after this.

"I must say, I wish I had been given elocution lessons. My parents didn't even let me have speech therapy. You know the King was treated by a speech therapist who did wonders for him. When I was nineteen years old speech therapy wasn't even recognised as it is now. Tell me why you think you were unsuccessful [he had some difficulty with that word] in obtaining a place at the other medical schools when you started out? You could have tried Glasgow, you know."

Izzy took this as a hint, he was feeling more confident now, and he gently broached the subject of his religious origins.

"Oh, I expect that you think that it was anti-Semitism. I have had a few applicants complain about that when they couldn't get a place here, but you can't say that I'm anti-Semitic, can you, eh?" Izzy decided to take a more placatory tone and agreed. The Dean went on,

"You have probably heard of my brother. He was a Cambridge graduate like myself and a fine athlete. He suffered a bit but he chose to ignore it and he has done quite well. He represented our country and has won all sorts of medals." Izzy did not know this but he nodded his head in agreement.

There was a pregnant pause and to Izzy's horror the man in whom he had placed so much hope shuffled the papers on his desk and almost casually in a rather off hand dismissive manner said,

"Look here, I can't give you a place here. We have only a few left and if I take you some of my colleagues might say that I am showing too much favour to my coreligionists. Even in my position, and I am not at all religious, I have to watch my Ps and Qs. My advice to you is to change your name. Lots of people do this in order to get on. Our Royal Family did it during the Great War. They had a German name but because we were fighting the Germans they changed it from Saxe-Coburg Gotha to Windsor. If they can do it so can you."

Izzy had difficulty in accepting this. After all, this man had a typically Jewish name himself.

The answer to this unasked question came spontaneously from the Dean.

"Oh, I know what you're thinking but what you must understand is that I was lucky. You could also say that I come from a privileged background. You don't. You want to get on. MacKay says that you are a good fellow. Look, I'll tell you what I'll do: Think of a new name over lunch, come back and see me at two o'clock and I'll write a note to Merrick who is Dean of the other medical school to which you have applied. He may take you, but in either case I suggest that your chances there would be better with another name. Think of another name yourself and come back this afternoon. You had better go now. It's getting late and I need my lunch, 'bye-'bye."

It was perhaps fortunate that the Dean did not notice the gore that rose in Izzy's throat at this last dismissive remark. He scurried out of the Dean's office vowing never to return. It was fortunate that Alf was waiting outside. He had never seen Izzy so angry. It took a pint of beer and some strong persuasive arguments from Alf to change Izzy's mind.

Reluctantly, Izzy did return at two o'clock.

"Don't sit down," the Dean said. "What's your new name going to be?"

"Henry Barker," answered Izzy. The Dean took out his fountain pen and wrote a letter in long hand. He read it out.

"Dear Merrick," it said. "Would you kindly admit my friend Henry Barker to your school. I would give him a place here, but he does not want to feel that a personal friendship should influence my admitting him. He is quite a good chap and I am sure that he will do well with you." He then inserted the letter in an envelope, sealed it, got up, shook Henry by the hand, wished him luck and showed him out. Henry never saw him again, but he did write him a fulsome letter of thanks. Later on, he met one of his successors. It was Jab.

This treasured epistle was delivered by hand to the secretary of the last remaining medical school where there was a possibility of admission. A new application form was filled out in the secretary's office, this time with the new name. Henry left the office feeling that this was his last and only chance, but his hopes were high.

He was called for interview a few days later. It was brief. Merrick was brisk. He was a blunt Yorkshireman.

"Oh, so you're a friend of Adolph's, are you? How is he these days? By the way, you don't live in a very good area. Tell me why is that? Do you come from a medical family?"

Henry was a little overwhelmed by this and decided to lie.

"My sister and I lost our parents a few years ago. My father was a gentleman farmer and when he died he left us both in rather reduced circumstances, I am afraid."

"All right, then...," was Merrick's response, "All right then. Start next Wednesday."

Never Read Someone Else's Correspondence

It was a pleasant, summer afternoon in June 1977. My neighbour Frank leant over the garden wall and asked me what the hypothalamus was. He was not a doctor so I explained to him that it is a small centre at the base of the brain that controls certain bodily functions, such as temperature, blood pressure, growth, etc.

"Have you ever come across a patient with a tumour of the hypothalamus?" he asked. I told him I had, and that the previous chief had been the first person to describe the disease.

"Yes," said Frank. "We have written to him but he doesn't seem able to help. But the staff of a well-known Children's' hospital said that they would do a brain scan to see whether the tumour was present or not."

"What's the problem?" I said.

"Well, the patient is my cousin's, cousin's daughter. He is a Professor of Chemistry in Moscow. Katrina, who is only nine years old, is always getting fevers for which they have found no cause, and she is wasting away, will not eat, and has stopped growing. She went to a paediatrician in Moscow who diagnosed this disease. The parents asked whether anything could be done, but the paediatrician said that he did not think so.

"The father wrote to one of the doctors at a well-known Children's hospital in London, because the condition could only be diagnosed with a brain scan. At this time the only two instruments in the world were in London, and he thought that it was not unreasonable for the child to come here to be investigated. They also went to another paediatrician in Kiev in the Ukraine to get a second opinion. She had agreed with her colleague in Moscow. Unfortunately when the Paediatrician in Moscow got to hear of this he was annoyed, not at all helpful, and would not continue care. Both parents became dissidents and applied to leave the Soviet Union. The staff at the children's hospital in London will see her and treat her free but she cannot leave the country. All sorts of people have written to the Soviet Embassy in London and a lot of representation has been made but this seems to be of no use. He is in a desperate situation now because he has lost his job at the research institute and is finding it difficult to survive. His wife has lost her job and they are living in someone else's flat. He managed to speak to his cousin a professor of computing in Philadelphia, who has written to me about it. Meanwhile, the child is wasting away, having these high temperatures and the whole situation is a very unhappy one. Do you think you could help?"

I pondered the matter and felt that I couldn't, but suggested that the father write to me from Moscow and send more details. I might think of something or possibly be able to influence someone else, or other people in this country, but the outlook seemed hopeless.

I did actually receive a letter from the cousin in Philadelphia. It explained the situation fully, and some six weeks later I actually received a letter from the father in Moscow. This contained further details of the case, and temperature charts that he had been taking himself. The fever was intermittent, lasting for a week at a time, and there had been some weight loss. The description of the child was rather an emotional one, but I felt sorry for the man and understood the difficult predicament he was in. His letter was addressed to me at one of my hospitals. When I read it I imparted the contents to my secretary, Julia. She made a very good suggestion.

"Why don't you write to Mr Smith (that is not his name)? If you remember he works at the Foreign Office. You know him reasonably well and he has lots of connections. He may be able to help the child." I thought that a handwritten letter would be the best thing, and filled up two sides explaining the situation. I received a reply within three days. This was also handwritten. He wrote that he would do what he could but the situation looked hopeless. However, two weeks later we had another letter from him. Somehow he had been able to use his influence and he wrote to let me know that if the said professor in chemistry were to go to the British Embassy in Moscow he would receive visas for his whole family to come to this country. I immediately sent a letter to him in Moscow explaining this. I did not receive a reply from Moscow, despite sending two more letters, and only heard some two months later saying that he had eventually received news from his cousin in Philadelphia, to whom I had already written. He was most grateful. He had been to the British Embassy in Moscow and had indeed obtained the visas. Unfortunately, his daughter Katrina's condition had deteriorated further.

I showed this letter to Julia, my secretary. I had slit it open, but she noticed that the flap had previously already been steamed open. It was Passover time and after our usual prayers for Soviet Jewry I read out several of our refusnik's letters to the people round the table and made a special prayer for the child.

I did not hear from them for some time, and had no replies to several letters even after writing to his cousin in Philadelphia. I discussed the matter with Frank, my neighbour. We seemed to have come to a stop. Things were frustrating. Nine months had now gone by.

Some six weeks later I received a heart-rending letter from Moscow saying that the visas would soon run out, there had been no progress and his daughter's condition was getting much worse. I had to think of something.

Now, many years ago my wife's father had had something to do with the early career of a very prominent member of the Cabinet. This man's wife was actually Chairman of the Board of Governors of the Children's Hospital that had offered free treatment to the child. It occurred to me that were I to write to her, and explain the relationship that her husband had with my late father-in-law, and tell her that the Foreign Office had already arranged for visas, she might be able to exert some influence with the Soviet authorities. I did so, and enclosed copies of the correspondence. I awaited a reply but heard nothing for three weeks. However, on a Saturday morning I was gratified to receive a letter which came from the Cabinet Office in Downing Street. My wife was all agog. I opened it with trepidation that evening only to find that it was merely an acknowledgement of receipt of my letter, and nothing more. At this point it seemed that my efforts had been frustrated again but I thought about it over the weekend and on Monday morning decided to make a bold move.

I wrote another letter to the father in Moscow, and said that I had just heard from the Cabinet Office in London, and that he must be fully aware that the Foreign Office was interested in his case as they had provided visas. I wrote that I was worried, because I had now received a letter from the Prime Minister's Office and I was writing to let him know that people in high authority in this country were interested in his daughter's case. I realised that his correspondence was being interfered with in the Soviet Union and that it was likely that my letters to him were being stolen, opened or confiscated Should he not receive this letter or a copy which I would send him in two weeks, and if I did not receive an acknowledgement of this correspondence, then after another two weeks, I would personally complain to the powers that be. I was quite sure there would be trouble for those who had been interfering with the post in the Soviet Union.

I waited anxiously for another month but heard nothing, but then received a telephone call from my friend at the Foreign Office to say that he had just signed a letter which I would receive in a few days. This stated that the professor, his wife and daughter were going to be released from the Soviet Union and were coming to this country. He let me have the date, the time of the flight and the flight number and asked me to meet them at Heathrow Airport. I took the letter to my neighbour Frank, who hailed it with glee.

On the appointed day we both went to the airport to meet them. We waited and waited until apparently everybody had alighted from the plane and gone through customs, but our family did not appear. I was sure that they must have arrived. Armed with the letter from the Foreign Office and with a little persuasion I was allowed to enter the Customs Hall. The family was there. Their luggage was being thoroughly searched. I explained the situation to the Custom Officers and showed them the letters. They stopped their search and released the father, mother, and child.

We took them to the tea bar for refreshment. It was an emotional moment for all of us. They had arrived with all their worldly possessions contained in three suitcases. They had been expelled and were not allowed to return to the Soviet Union ever again. When they had settled down over a cup of tea, I told them that I had written them two letters in the previous six weeks, and asked why there was no reply. The answer was that my letters had never been received.

They must have arrived because the professor told me that he was suddenly summoned to an office in Moscow and told that he had to get out of the country quickly. Apparently, a British delegation from the Foreign Office was shortly going to visit Moscow and one of the officials seemed to think that someone in England might cause trouble. They released our professor his wife and daughter presumably after intercepting and reading my letters.

The child had the scan – there was no tumour present. She certainly had severe chronic sinusitis that responded to standard treatment. She has had no further fevers and is now well. Her father is doing very good research at a famous scientific institute.

I rarely see them these days and hope that I have given the correct interpretation of the events of the time. It does go to show that on no account should one read someone else's private correspondence without permission!.

Feets

It was one of our duties as students to attend the accident and emergency [A&E] department and sit in on the consultations with one of the junior doctors who worked there. One of these was very popular. The story was that by some detective work he had discovered the source of infection with gonorrhoea of five young men who at different times had attended the A & E with this embarrassing condition. By close and perhaps not entirely professional questioning of three of them, he had discovered the name and telephone number of the young woman from whom they had received her unprofessional favours and incidentally had become infected. The young casualty doctor had persuaded them to confront her and if necessary bring her along to the venereal department and get her treated. This they did with some success, and the story quickly travelled round the hospital making the young doctor something of a popular hero.

When Joe, Harry and Jeff attended the A&E they were unlucky. Their hero was not on duty. They knew who was in charge. They also knew that he was the son of one of the senior consultants and it was generally suspected that his unimpeded and rapid postgraduate professional progress had been aided by paternal influence. He was by no means one of the brightest members of the junior staff.

They took their seats in his small office and awaited the first patient. This turned out to be a greying middle-aged Polish man. He was untidily dressed but on his left lapel was displayed the bars of several medals. Joe recognised the Africa Star among them.

"What is your problem?", was the first question.

The reply was simple, "With the feets."

The young doctor turned to Joe and asked him to classify epilepsy. He seemed dissatisfied when he received the right answer.

Returning to the patient he questioned him further.

"Do you know that you are going to get one?" He asked.

The patient looked a little bemused, and replied that he had them,"… all the time."

It was now Harry's turn. He was asked the stages of epileptic fit. He got the answer right.

The questioner asked about the first stage or aura and the various types including unusual tastes or smells.

The patient interrupted,

"Yes I have ze problem with the smells." The interrogator smiled and now turning to Jeff asked him which type of convulsive disorder was associated with abnormal smells.

Jeff's reply was prompt.

"This was uncinate lobe epilepsy first described by Hughlings Jackson in 18.....". He was cut short and told that he knew too much for his own good. He went on. "Treatment is important. I am going to ask the patient what he has been taking for these strange attacks. What medicines are you taking my man?"

"I take little round pills and a powder that the doctor in the Polish Army used to give me. Can I have some more?"

"Bah! Continental medicine! Powders for epilepsy indeed! We no longer use powders! This is the 20th Century my man. Incidentally, how do you take them?"

"I also have ointment."

"Ointment for epilepsy, indeed this gets worse! Where do you apply it? To your head?

"No sir, on ze feets. Zat is ze problem I came here for. Ze feets they smell."

The students were convulsed with laughter. They could not hold back any longer.

"Get out!" was the response from their erstwhile tutor.

Happily, they left.